#7 in the Scott Moss Detective Series

Who's at the Bottom
of the River?

Ross Van Dusen

ii

Chapter 1
Something Bad Is Going To Happen

"So where are we going on our honeymoon, Scott?" Julia Weston-Moss asked.

"I thought you wanted our destination to be a surprise," Scott answered.

"I did, but we're on our way to LAX. So you can tell me now." She and Scott Moss had been married for a little over sixteen hours.

Scott smiled. "Not yet."

"It better not be Panama," she cautioned. "I had enough *fun* the last time we went there."

"No. Far from it."

"Good." Julia sat back. After a minute she asked, "Europe?"

"No. Far from there, too."

"So, what? We're going to Siberia?"

"Not there, either," Scott said with a smile.

Julia thought about it for a moment and then closed her eyes. "Where the hell are we going, Scott, Australia?" She paused. "It better not be someplace goofy . . . like Gary, Indiana."

"Which airline?" the cabbie asked.

"Alaska Air," Scott said with a grin.

"Oh, good grief! I didn't bring clothes for dog sledding, Scott. The photos you showed me didn't have any outdoorsy outfits at all."

Scott laughed. "It's summer there too, Jules. And we're going to be safe and warm on one of those riverboat cruises. You know—they go up those inland rivers and stuff."

"And stuff? How much research did you put into this, Scott? When you cut out those pictures to show me what kind of clothes to bring they were mostly dinner clothes and walk around the plaza clothes. I only have a lightweight jacket to wear in the evening. I didn't even bring a sweater to wear if it gets chilly."

"We'll buy you a sweater if you need one. Don't worry, we'll buy anything we need. It's very cosmopolitan up there. They have stores, and running water, and electricity."

"Right. And igloos and polar bears."

"It's a riverboat. There won't be any bears."

The cabbie pulled up. "Forty-two fifty. You two kids have a nice honeymoon. I hear the mosquitoes up there are so big they carry the little children off to feast on them."

"Thanks a lot," Scott groaned.

Julia gave them both a wary frown. "How often do we have to leave this riverboat?"

"Hey, Jules, we can stay in the room for the entire honeymoon if you want. Isn't that what newlyweds are supposed to do? I've seen it in the movies. They put a 'Do Not Disturb' sign

2

on the door and don't come out for two weeks." He paused. "I think I'd like room service once in a while, though."

Scott and the cabbie grinned while Julia rolled her eyes. "We've been living together for two years, Scott. I'm not spending five days in a room with you. You're too . . ."

"Too what?"

". . . We're too old for that. And you're too *you* for that."

"They're called cabins," the cabbie said.

"You stay out of this," Julia warned.

The cabbie kept his eyes forward to hide his amusement and whispered, "Okay."

"The cabin better be nice. And there better be a really nice dining room on this riverboat, with really fancy food, very nice wines, and a dance floor for dancing, or you're in big trouble."

"Uh-oh, I went for the wiener cruise. We get two hammocks, a shared bathroom, and all the beer and hot dogs we can eat."

"Not funny."

Scott stared out the side window. "The brochure said gourmet food. How about dining and looking out the windows at the glaciers and stuff? I'm not much of a dancer."

"Ohh, no, you're dancing." She paused. "And I thought the glaciers all melted."

"Not yet. That's why we're going there. We can tell our children we saw the remnants of the big freeze. Or, maybe we should call it the big melt. Either way, we'll put the last tiny chunk of

3

glacier in the freezer and show it to them when they grow up. Then we'll put it in a glass of vodka and drink to the end of an era."

"It's called global warming," Julia said.

"Which is going to cause everything to melt. Hence the big melt." Scott answered.

"It's all gonna freeze again, you know. In a thousand years," the cabbie said.

"In a thousand years I won't care," Scott said.

"In the meantime, I don't have a sweater to wear tonight," Julia complained.

Scott dropped his head. "Jeez."

~~~~~~~~~~

Jason Fellows wheeled his wife, Joyce, through the Denver Airport. "Where are we going, Jason? I didn't get a chance to tell my friends anything. You said Michigan, but now we're going to Alaska?"

"I have business there, Joyce. I had to change our plans. I booked a river cruise—we need to get away from all this legal trouble."

"God is punishing me."

"Yeah, me too," Jason mumbled as he pushed her wheelchair to the gate.

~~~~~~~~~~

The cab driver took the Mosses' two suitcases out of the trunk. Scott gave the cabbie fifty-five dollars and dragged their two bags and his photo bag to the Alaska Air counter. "You'll be fine, Jules. It's summertime up there too, it'll be nice and warm, relax."

"It's late summer at best—fall, really. And it would have been nice if you had shown me one picture with a walrus or a seal in it, just to give me a heads-up."

~~~~~~~~~~~

Jason Fellows slid his United Airlines tickets across the counter. "Here you are."

The United gal checked them in. "Have a nice flight, Mr. and Mrs. Butane."

"What?" Joyce said as Jason quickly wheeled her away from the check-in. "Mrs. Butane?"

"It's nothing, Joyce. With all the legal troubles we have, I decided to travel under a different name, that's all. Those lawyers don't need to know our every move, do they?"

"I'm so sorry, Jason." Joyce put her head in her hands. "This is all my fault."

"Yeah well . . . buck up," Jason angrily said.

~~~~~~~~~~~

Scott slapped their tickets on the airline counter. "You have a point. But oddly enough, there weren't any pictures of animals in the brochure, or I might have."

"Might have? Oh, that's comforting." Julia noticed the gal behind the counter reading something from under their tickets and then quickly hiding it. "What was that? What was that paper you just hid?"

"Nothing, *Miss*. Have a nice flight—and have a very nice honeymoon," the girl answered.

Scott winked at her, and whisked Julia away from the counter.

"What was that note you gave her? What did it say?" Julia asked, as Scott pulled her down the concourse. She kept looking back. "And why did she call me *miss* in such a pronounced manner? What's going on, Scott?"

"The note didn't *say* anything—it's a note. I wrote we're on our honeymoon. I thought you might be pleased if she wished us a happy honeymoon on our way."

Julia thought about it while Scott dragged her to the security check. Her lawyer instincts were in play. They got to the large scanner and Julia stepped in. "What else did you say—write?" she asked as the machine scanned her body.

"Smile, Jules." Scott took her photo with her arms up. "What else would I write? I just wrote to say happy honeymoon. Scott was next to be swept. "Step through, Jules. It's my turn."

Julia put her hands on her hips, turned and demanded, "What else did you write, Scott?"

"Okay, please step through." The checker waited, but Julia stood, defiantly, with her hands still on her hips. "Step through," he repeated.

Julia ignored him. "What did you tell her—I mean write to her in that note, Scott?" Julia sounded fierce.

"Nothing," Scott said, and took another shot. He turned to the woman behind him. "This is her first time flying. She's afraid of airplanes."

The woman dropped her eyes.

Julia wasn't moving out of the body scanner. "You had her call me *miss*, didn't you!"

"Ma'am, please move through. You're okay," the checker said.

Julia turned and glared at the man. "I guess you didn't get a note. It's *Mrs.* now, dammit." Julia moved on grumbling, "You're supposed to be fifty pounds overweight and fifty years old to be called *ma'am*."

"Sorry," the man mumbled.

Julia marched on. "Yeah, right."

Scott stepped in and held his arms up. The machine scanned him as he turned and said, "I screwed up," to the woman behind him. "Not a good start to our honeymoon." She snapped her head down once more, avoiding eye contact. "Don't worry. These fancy machines won't contaminate us," Scott said to her. "I may never be able to have children, though."

Again, the woman quickly stared at her shoes, avoiding eye contact.

Scott stepped through to an angry Julia. He gave a quick look back at the woman behind him as he said, "Don't be mad, Jules. We're on our honeymoon." He looked back at the woman one more time.

Julia sighed, "You're right. I shouldn't be so sensitive. Now that I'm an old married woman."

The bag checker set Scott's camera bag aside. "I'm afraid you'll have to show me that these cameras work, sir."

Scott quickly took a photo with each of his three cameras and showed the images to the checker. "See? They're really cameras—I'm a photographer now."

"Now?" the checker asked.

"I used to be a private detective. Actually, I still am. Long story. The photo business isn't as lucrative as you might imagine. So I kinda still do both. Okay, hold it." He took the checker's photograph. "I'll send you a copy when we get back from our honeymoon."

"Yeah, terrific. You can go on," the man said and waved him through. "Step through if you please—thank you.

Scott could tell Julia was still slightly miffed. "You still got it, kid," he reassured, and then checked the woman behind him one more time.

"Really, Scott? I've still got it? Then why are you checking out that lady behind you? Please don't tell me you've developed a wandering eye before the honeymoon has even started."

"Wandering eye? She's at least ten years older than me." Scott put his shoes back on.

"Than I," Julia mumbled.

"No. Something about her seems a little off." He watched the woman slip her shoes back on. "I can't tell what it is but it's off."

"Here we go," Julia threw her hands up and slapped them down on her thighs.

"Here we go, where?"

"Somebody's going to die on our honeymoon."

"We don't know that."

"Somebody's going to get kidnapped."

"We don't know that."

"Shot."

"We don't know . . ."

"Stabbed."

"We don't . . ."

"Thrown overboard."

Scott paused. "Now, that could happen."

"Not funny, Scott."

As they boarded the plane, Scott noticed that the woman who followed him through the scanner kept her head down and nearly ran to the very back row of seats. They buckled up, took off, and ten minutes into the flight, Scott said, "I'm going to the bathroom," and started for the back of the plane.

Julia pointed. "There's one right up in front, Scott. It's much closer."

"That's okay. I like to pee in the back. That way nobody can see me come out of the can. I'm very shy about things like that." He headed down the aisle, ignoring the frown of the man sitting directly behind them.

9

Julia shook her head and said, "Shy, my Aunt Fanny. You're very nosy. I saw that lady go to the back of the plane." She sighed deeply, rifled the seat pocket and thumbed through the in-flight magazine. "This is going to end badly—very badly. I just know it."

The woman buried her head in her in-flight magazine when he approached. "Hmmm," he said as he opened the lavatory door.

Two minutes later, when he came out, she stuck her head back in the magazine. Scott's antenna was on full alert. "The woman I checked out behind us is trying to be invisible," he said when he got back to his seat.

Julia closed her eyes. "Every time. Every time we do anything, something happens."

"Oh, come on, that's not true. Our wedding went off without a hitch."

"My minister got stabbed!" she hollered.

The lady in the seat in front of them heard Julia, jumped, and looked horrified.

"Well, yeah, but that was long before we got hitched," Scott defended. "I mean after that. The actual ceremony."

"We had to wait almost two months for him to recover! And you got shot again! That's why we just got married yesterday! Instead of in the middle of May or in early June as I'd hoped." She was still incensed.

The lady in front of them turned her ear to hear their conversation.

"That was just a scrape from some glass."

"That was a bullet wound. I'm not stupid."

The lady pressed her ear closer.

"Don't be mad, Jules. It isn't my fault. It's just that the woman who was behind me in line is calling attention to herself by trying to *not* call attention to herself."

"Something only you would notice." Julia stared out at the clouds. "I don't know why I thought this would be any different. Something bad is going to happen, and we're going to be right in the middle of it."

"I know, I know, I shouldn't. But she's acting really weird, Jules."

"You know you shouldn't, so don't, Scott."

"Do you think she has a bomb in her shoe?"

"What!" The passenger in front of them snapped around in her seat.

"No, no. We were talking about that guy in Detroit. It was years ago," Scott assured.

The lady turned back around and Julia said, "That was the underwear guy, Scott."

"Unimportant detail,"

They flew in silence for almost an hour. Julia finally said, "You know, I feel . . . different. I know we've been together a long time, but I'm actually excited about our new status."

"Did you bring a honeymoon nightie?"

Julia smiled. "I did, actually. One you've never seen before."

"Oh, that's outstanding," Scott said, with a big grin. "I love those kind of surprises." He noticed the lady in front of them had perked up.

"It shouldn't be all on me, you know. What did you bring for me? Anything interesting?" Julia teased, knowing he would only bring his blue button-down shirts, a few pairs of Dockers, changes of underwear, socks, and no jammies. Plus his ever-present camera bag.

Scott could tell that the passenger in front of them was still listening. "Oh, I brought the usual. Ropes, handcuffs, a ball gag." He paused. "The leather hoist wouldn't fit in my bag. But hey, we'll figure something out."

In front of them, the lady's eyes bugged out.

Scott pointed to her and then to his ear. It was for her benefit.

Julia pointed her two fingers like a gun at Scott and dropped her thumb. Then she put on a neck pillow and closed her eyes.

"I thought it was funny," Scott whispered.

"You think everything you say is funny." She nestled in. "But it's not."

Hours later they landed and picked up their luggage. Quite a few people on the flight loaded onto the special bus that would take them to the riverboat. Scott kept half an eye out for the mysterious passenger from the flight. She waited on the fringes of the activity then slipped on the riverboat bus at the very last second and went directly to the back seat.

Scott nudged Julia. "The mystery woman got on our bus, Jules. And I didn't see her leave any luggage in the bin thing."

"Dammit!" Julia closed her eyes again. After a minute she started to get up.

"Where are you going?" Scott asked.

"We're not getting on that boat," she said. "This is how it always starts. She's going to kill someone, or someone is going to kill her, or kidnap her, or blow up the boat, or she's going to blow something up. And you're going to be right in the middle of it."

Julia struggled to get up but Scott gently held her back. "Come on, Jules, nothing's going to happen. Please sit down."

"Are you kidding? Our honeymoon is going to be a murder investigation. There's going to be badges and bodies and bad guys everywhere. It's going to be just like everything else we do."

"Be sitting and staying and sweet . . . ing everywhere." Scott held her arm. "Please?"

"Sweeting?" Julia stared at him and frowned. "What's the matter with you?"

"You did *B*'s, so I did *S*'s."

Julia tried to get up. "Not funny." Before she could get away, the bus driver closed the door, smiled, and said, "I hope everyone's ready for a really wonderful, and truly unforgettable trip."

"You don't know the half of it, buddy boy," Julia blurted out, then covered her mouth with her hands. "Oops."

"It's okay. She's afraid of boats," Scott said to the concerned couple across the aisle.

"Am not," she mumbled. "I'm afraid of you."

A short bus ride later, they boarded the small, hundred-passenger riverboat. Scott and Julia stood in the door of their stateroom. It was beautiful—a sitting room, a large bedroom, a very nice bathroom, and two very large windows overlooking the port. "Wow. Pretty nice, huh, Jules? Now I'm *really* glad I opted out of the wiener cruise."

The luxury was softening Julia's attitude. "It really is, Scott. I just hope this doesn't end up like it did in Panama."

"Hey! Whoa. Nothing happened on the ship to Panama. It was the best trip we ever had."

Julia didn't look convinced. "You got shot in Panama. You almost died."

"But nothing happened on the cruise, right? It happened after we made port in Panama. And we don't even have to get off the riverboat on this trip if we don't want to, right? Besides, there aren't any kidnappers running around loose, like there were back then, right? There aren't any killers or anything, right?"

"Right." Julia started unpacking, but it was clear she wasn't convinced.

"Let's go wander the deck. I'd like to take a few photos and get a feel for the ship, okay?"

"Sure, let me just get my sweater. Oh, that's right. I don't have a sweater."

"It's seventy degrees out there!"

"It's sixty-eight." Julia picked up her purse and Scott grabbed a camera. They wandered the deck while the last of the passengers boarded.

Scott took a few shots of the boarding process. He shot the crew loading provisions, large flat pushcarts loaded with fresh fruits and vegetables; he photographed passengers trying to find their cabins, wandering the deck, looking lost. And he got a great shot of a couple arguing over their cabin's small size.

"Good thing you can't see ours." He mumbled.

Very late in the boarding process, Jason Fellows pushed his wife on, in her wheelchair. Scott took a photo, and Julia took note of them. She suddenly took Scott's hand. "Ohhh, that's nice. That's really sweet, isn't it? I wonder how long they've been together?"

"The last one standing pushes the other one, okay?" he whispered.

Julia squeezed Scott's hand. "You bet."

The lifeboat drill took place thirty minutes later. Scott took a shot of the sea of orange life jackets, and looked for the invisible woman. "Hey, Jules, keep an eye out for that mystery passenger from the flight, okay?"

"What does she look like?"

"Her face looks like the front and back of the in-flight magazine."

Julia shook her head. "Ohh, wonderful. She'll be easy to spot."

Scott scanned everyone. "I'm looking, but I don't think she's here."

"So? She's at the other station—at the front of the boat."

When the drill was over, Scott ran to the front of the boat to check for her, but the passengers had already scattered.

Julia caught up to him. "It's a pretty small boat, we'll come across her eventually."

"What? Now the boat's not big enough?"

"No . . . I wasn't . . . ohh, nuts to you." Julia said when she realized he was pulling her chain.

Chapter 2
What Was That Splash?

As the boat left port, Scott looked around for the mystery woman. She was nowhere on deck. "Do you see our Nervous Nelly anywhere?"

"Pick a name, Scott. Is she invisible, or mystery, or nervous. I need to know what, or whom, you're talking about."

"I pick Nelly."

"Oh, terrific. And her face looks like the cover of the in-flight magazine. How am I supposed to recognize her, Scott?"

"I don't know." Scott shrugged. "She looks a lot like the woman we saw in the wheelchair—same hair and everything. Just keep an eye out for a single woman walking around, okay?"

"I take it back. Trouble doesn't follow you, you go looking for it."

"You can't take it back, Jules. You didn't throw anything out there."

"Scott, I'm not going to enjoy any part of this honeymoon because you're already making me nervous about some woman who didn't do anything except be a little nervous herself. Maybe she's nervous because she's never traveled alone before. Could we please not do this? Okay?"

"Okay, okay. I'm sorry. Let's forget it."

"I will if you will."

"I promise."

"Yeah, right."

Julia watched the port slip behind them. The boat sailed into wilderness almost immediately. "That was quick. I guess they don't have very big suburbs up here in Alaska."

"I guess not." Scott took photos down the length of the boat. He shot passengers' heads and arms hanging out over the rail, gawking and pointing. He got a shot of a yacht going the other way, people waving. He got permission to shoot the engine room. He caught passengers drinking at the deckside bar. After a while, Julia went to their cabin, finished unpacking, took a long shower, and a short nap.

When she returned, Scott had put away his cameras. "Let's get a drink in the bar," he said.

"Tired of the scenery already? We have five days of this ahead of us, Scott. Are you sure you've thought this through?"

"No, no, it's beautiful—all the trees and bushes and stuff. I just thought we could look at it while we have a drink in the bar. You know, looking out the window . . . and having a drink."

"You don't have to get me drunk, Scott, you married me—I'm yours." Julia gave Scott a wry look. "You just have to make tonight the most romantic night of my life."

The couple next to them perked up.

"Holy wedding vows! Now *I'm* getting nervous. I don't know if I'll be able to live up to most romantic night of your life. That's a tall order."

The couple next to Scott and Julia had their ears turned toward them, listening. They smiled.

Julia leaned over to them. "I'm a virgin," she said, shyly.

The man reddened, and his wife quickly pulled him away, saying, "I'm sorry. We didn't mean to invade your privacy,"

"Bye," Scott said and led the way to the bar.

Julia pointed out the window as they entered the room. "Oh look, bushes and stuff." She gave Scott a jab, and sat in the corner booth.

Scott ordered a bottle of champagne, and after a glass and a half, everything was smoothed over. Julia let go of her angst and watched the sun wink at them through the peaks and crevices. After a bit, she said, "It's so nice here I don't feel like moving. Let's just have a light dinner in the bar, okay?"

"You got it," Scott said.

The ship's address system came on. "Will the person who removed the twenty-pound weights from the exercise room please put them back. The weights are for everyone, and not to be used in your cabin. Thank you for your cooperation."

"I bet it's some shy fatty," Scott said.

After they finished the champagne, they had a very nice steak dinner with a very nice red wine.

After a brandy nightcap, they headed to their cabin. "You know what? I have to hand it to you, Scott." Julia hugged his arm. "This is much more romantic than I thought it would be."

Scott patted her hand. "Glad you're enjoying it, Mrs. Weston-Moss."

"You know, that sounds kind of weird on our honeymoon. I can be just plain old Mrs. Moss when I'm not doing lawyer things."

"You got it, Sugar lips."

"Don't care for nick-names, Scott."

"Okay, Mrs. Moss."

"Jules or Julia would be nice."

"Okay Jules or Julia."

"Not funny."

~~~~~~~~~~

Julia's honeymoon nightie made Scott forget all about the mysterious passenger. They turned out the lights, made love—once with the nightie on, and once with the nightie off—and then talked well into the night. They were still talking at three in the morning when Scott heard a splash. "Did you hear that?" He went to the window and pressed the darkness. "It sounded like something just made a big splash against the boat, or maybe some big fish jumped in the water."

Julia rolled over on her back and mumbled, "It was the predictable murder, Scott. By tomorrow morning you'll be up to your armpits in a crime and our honeymoon will be over."

"Maybe we hit a walrus."

"Maybe it'll rain gumdrops. Come to bed."

"Hey Jules, you should see the stars. It's so dark it looks like there's a gazillion of them."

"There *are* a gazillion of them. Don't you ever watch Nova?" She got up, looked out, and hugged Scott at the window. "Oh my God. That's amazing. I've never seen them so sharp and so bright. You can actually see them twinkling."

"Light pollution in LA. We would never see them like this at home."

After a few minutes she said, "Come to bed. I don't want to miss breakfast." Julia slipped under the covers. "Come on, Scott, it's past three in the morning and breakfast ends at ten."

Scott gave the sky one last look, glanced at the water, thought a little about the splash, shook his head, and climbed into bed.

~~~~~~~~~~

They got up late and wandered into the dining room just in time. It was the last half hour of the breakfast seating. "Can we get something by the window?" Scott asked.

"Absolutely," the waiter said, and led them over to a booth at a big window.

Julia checked the menu.1 "I'll have the eggs Florentine and tea," Julia said. "And some milk for the tea, please."

"I'll have the same," Scott said. "But instead of spinach under those eggs could you slip in a nice

21

piece of Canadian bacon,? And instead of tea, make it coffee with cream instead of milk. Thanks."

"Sure. One Florentine with tea, one Florentine Benedict Arnold with coffee, coming right up," the waiter said. "Any juice?"

"Orange juice, please."

"And for the gentleman?"

"I'll have the same, but make it a grapefruit juice," Scott said.

"One OJ, one GJ, coming up." The waiter left.

"Ohh, I'm gonna like him," Scott whispered, "He doesn't rattle."

At the last possible minute, Jason Fellows, with his wife in the wheelchair, rolled in and found a window booth, across the dining room from them.

Scott and Julia noticed but paid no attention— until Jason's wife got up and sat in the booth, while Jason collapsed the wheelchair and leaned it against the wall. "It looks like she can walk a little bit," Scott observed.

"Very interesting." Julia glanced over every few minutes, until their breakfasts came. "Ohh, these look wonderful, thank you," she said.

"Will there be anything else?" the waiter asked.

"No, we're good. Thanks." Scott dug right in.

Julia started to eat, but kept looking toward the woman from the wheelchair.

"What's up, Jules?" Scott looked over. "Did you expect him to eat alone? Or did you think he'd murdered her already?" He took another bite of his breakfast. "Perfect! The eggs are perfect."

Julia stopped for a beat. "She looks different. I can't put my finger on it, but something's different about her this morning."

Scott looked over. "Really? Different—how? We only saw her for two seconds."

"I don't know. I must be seeing things." Julia shrugged it off and went back to her breakfast.

Halfway through breakfast, Scott signaled for more coffee and Julia looked at the woman again. "Do you want to go over and make friends, Jules?" Scott waited for the waiter to pour him more coffee, and then said, "I'm not real big on chatting up strangers, but if it's really bugging you, we can go over and say hello."

"No. That would be the exact wrong thing to do. But, something's really strange about them."

"Ohhh, wow! I'm usually the one getting all squirrelly over things. You're creeping me out a little, Jules." Scott looked over one more time. "I took a photo of them when they came on board. Maybe we should check it out?"

"No, no, don't bother. I don't know what it is."

"So you said."

Breakfast over, Scott started to get up. "Sit!" Julia commanded. "Let's have a little more coffee."

"You had tea."

"So, now I'll have a cup of coffee, okay?" Julia quietly growled.

Scott waved the waiter over again, pointing at their cups. The waiter brought hot water and coffee.

"Just coffee this time," Scott said, "My wife just remembered she doesn't like tea."

"Don't listen to him," Julia said, "He's insane."

"I'm insane? You're the one chasing Lupin."

The waiter smirked. He knew about Lupin.

"Who?" Julia asked.

Scott smiled. "Unimportant detail."

The waiter retrieved a fresh cup and poured their coffees. When he left, Scott asked, "What's up Jules? You're giving me goose bumps."

"I don't know exactly. But I have kind of a weird feeling about them. Let's just wait until they leave," she said, not looking up.

"You don't know what it is, but you're going to find out. Damn, this is exciting." Scott whispered, "Are we going to follow them when they leave?"

"Of course we are. Before you became a photographer didn't you used to be a detective of some sort? A flatfoot or something?"

"Ohh, that's harsh. And I renewed my PI license a little while ago, remember? So I still am a *private investigator*, if you please."

"Like I said, a flatfoot. So you should know what happens next."

"Yeah, but I'm usually on the other end. I'm always trying to get you to go along, right?"

"So, now you know how it feels."

"No, no, I love it! This is great. A little silly, but great. Lead on, Mrs. Weston-Moss Holmes. Take us to the den of Arséne Lupin."

"Again—who?"

"Lupin—Sherlock's nemesis—it's a game."

Julia stared at Scott. "I pretty sure Sherlock's nemesis was Moriarty?"

"Him too. This is your case, Jules. I can't wait to see where it takes us."

"They're leaving. Get ready."

Scott said, "I was born ready," and snickered.

"Worst movie line ever." Julia threw her napkin on her plate and got up. She watched in her mirror, pretending to put on lipstick.

"Ahh! The old fake lipstick in the mirror trick."

"Don't start."

"I didn't start, you did."

"Okay, then stop."

They waited for the woman to get seated in her wheelchair and followed at a distance. "You don't think we'll lose them, do you, Jules?"

"Very funny. They'll be impossible to lose— there's only one wheelchair on this boat."

"That we know of."

Julia jabbed Scott with her elbow.

"This is a lark," Scott said.

"I'm so glad you're amused."

They followed the couple to their stateroom, took note of the number, and went on by. "Now what?" Scott asked.

"Now we wait," Julia said.

"Second worst movie line ever," Scott said. "Are we waiting for the stateroom to blow up, or for blood to run out from under the door, or what?"

"I don't know what. Stop making fun of me."

"Sorry."

"No you're not."

"So what do we do now, just run in place?"

"Sort of. We keep an eye on them. But we do it subtly, the way you watch a teenager. We'll keep track of where they go and what they do until I can figure out what it is they're really doing."

"Whoa! You never mentioned you have a teenager? In two years you never mentioned that." Scott frowned. "Did you fib a little on our marriage application, Jules? Am I stepdad to an evil little rascal that you keep hidden in a dark and damp basement somewhere?"

"Not funny." Julia shook her head. "We never should have gotten on this boat."

"Yeah, leaving that poor teenager alone in the basement was pretty cruel. I hope you left him, her, or it, some water at least."

"Not nice—or funny." But now Julia was fighting to stay serious. "It?" she mumbled.

~~~~~~~~~~~

The first stop was a little fishing village where all the tourists got to see skilled craftsmen carving totem poles in all sizes and browse through shops full of native carvings of all sorts.

Scott and Julia kept a loose eye on the mystery woman while they shopped. She was easy enough to spot in the small village. Every once in a while she would get up and walk past a few doors, then sit back down.

Scott was amused. "Look she can walk, she can walk! It's a miracle."

"Why is she using that chair? She doesn't look all that frail to me."

"Maybe she's just getting over an operation, or an accident. Lighten up, kid, we're on our romantic honeymoon, remember?"

"Sorry. I don't know what's bugging me. I get a little shiver every time I look at her."

"Here's a tip—don't look at her," Scott said. "Tell you what, I'll buy you the sweater you didn't bring. Then you won't shiver at all, okay?"

Julia suddenly stopped. "Her clothes don't fit. That's it. Oh my God, that's it."

"What?" Scott gave Julia a sideways glance, then checked the lady out. "She looks okay to me."

"They almost fit. But not quite."

Scott started laughing. "What does that mean? Maybe she just lost a lot of weight from some terrible disease and this is her recovery trip."

"You're right. I don't know why I'm getting so worked up about it." Julia shook her head. "Let's just forget about her."

"Good, let's get a coffee in that little shop on the corner. It smelled great when we passed by."

Scott and Julia and the hoard of people from the riverboat overwhelmed the little village for two or three hours and then headed back for dinner.

Most tourists had bags of souvenirs and clothing to bring back to the ship. Julia and Scott hadn't bought anything. Neither had the mystery couple. "What do you make of that, Jules? They're the only ones who didn't buy anything."

"Them and us," Julia said.

27

"They and we didn't buy," Scott answered.

"Yeah, I don't know why that sounds wrong. I guess it just does."

"Let's make a deal. We'll stop paying attention to them for the rest of the trip, okay?"

"I guess." Julia sounded resigned to the idea.

"Good! Let's head for the boat. All this not buying souvenirs has given me an appetite."

"I have to call my office when we get back to the ship. Then we can eat."

"Why don't you call now?" Scott asked.

"I'll want to take notes. It can wait."

"I should probably call Clair, too," Scott said.

"Right. You can tell her you have a new case. And I can tell you exactly what she'll say."

"What'll she say?"

"Some honeymoon."

"Okay, fifty bucks. But it has to be those exact words or you lose." Scott got on his phone.

"Make it five. Isn't that what our friend, Nick Scraper would say?" Julia asked.

"Hey, Clair, any messages?" Scott listened for a minute. "A missing school bus. Who would steal a school bus? What else? Another cheating husband." Scott sighed. "I'll take a pass on the husband. Can the school bus wait until we get back?" Scott shook his head. "Well, something's come up—up here. A man killed his wife, and Jules and I are going to catch the bastard." He flinched. "Dammit, Clair, you just cost me five bucks. I'll check in again in a few days. Thanks."

Julia grinned. "Told you."

28

"I need a new secretary. Someone who's way less predictable." Scott hung up.

She held out her hand. "Fork it over."

Scott dug into his Dockers. "Who would steal a school bus two days before school starts?"

"I don't know, the worst student?"

"Ohh!" Scott instantly got back on the phone. "Hey, Clair. Call the school people and tell them to check the back yards of their worst three students. Yes, it's brilliant. But it was Jules's idea. If they find it, tell them, no charge."

"Hey! I get nothing?"

"Well, lets see." Scott hesitated. "You get five more bucks. That's standard pay for brilliance." He pulled out another five.

"Huh," Julia said, staring at the bill. "You'd think brilliance would be worth a lot more than a measly five bucks."

Back at the riverboat, Julia called her office. Everything was under control. She tossed her pencil on the little nightstand. "Well, that was a pleasant surprise. We're good. Let's eat."

Dinner consisted of fresh-caught fish, baked and smothered in a sauce of crab and shrimp—served with fresh squash, an iceberg lettuce wedge covered with tiny bits of bacon, chopped egg, and capons, and drizzled with a semi-sweet dressing.

Everyone sat at the same table they took the first night, which put Scott and Julia across the dining room from their mystery couple.

Scott ate with gusto. "They *had* to serve iceberg lettuce, you know."

"Yes, I know." Julia smiled. "And I haven't had a wedge salad in forever. It's really great."

"And you know what they're going to serve for dessert, right?"

"Of course—baked Alaska."

"Elementary, Jules."

Julia couldn't help looking over.

"Hey. We're done with them, right?"

"Sorry." Julia looked out the window. It was just sunset. "My God, that's as beautiful as last night." She sighed. "I wasn't fully on board with this riverboat business at first, but it's been really wonderful, Scott. Thank you."

Dinner over, the dance floor was being cleared, a trio was setting up, and people were scattering. The mystery couple got up and the woman started to walk out. The man took her by the arm and quickly guided her back to the wheelchair.

Scott smiled, then frowned.

Julia watched Scott watch the couple. "You're feeling it too, aren't you?"

"Kinda, yeah." He stopped. "No. Hell no! This is your fault. You've got my imagination working overtime. They're just another couple."

"Still." Julia headed for the bar.

"Dammit, Jules." Scott chased after her. "This is silly. They're just like us."

"Okay."

"No, really. They are."

"Fine."

"Ahh, man. When you start answering me with one word answers I know something's wrong."

"Really?"

"See! See what you just did?"

"What?"

"One word answers. You're doing it to me like you do when I'm wrong and you're right."

"Really?"

"Now you're just playing with me."

"Am I?" Julia smugly said.

"Well, at least that was two words. And hell yes, you're playing with me."

They sat in a booth, and the waiter came over. "Good evening. What can I get you?"

"I'll have a vodka on the rocks. Jules?"

"A brandy, please."

"Me too. A brandy. Scratch the vodka rocks. I don't know what I was thinking."

Two brandies later they were in bed, looking out at the stars. "Do you think she just forgot to get back in her chair because she was feeling better? Or was—is—it something more sinister?" Julia asked.

"I think it's probably nothing," Scott said, "But since you brought it up; I haven't seen Nervous Nelly anywhere on the boat, have you?"

"No, I haven't." She paused. "What does Nelly have to do with wheelchair lady?"

"Nothing. It just popped into my head." Scott rolled over, then frowned. "*Why* did it just pop into my head? Was it because they look a lot alike? Is there—should there be some kind of connection?" Scott closed his eyes to go to sleep. A moment later he opened them, thought for a moment, and then

31

shook his head. "This is nuts, Jules. You've got me imagining things that aren't there."

"Uh-huh. It's just your imagination." Julia yawned and closed her eyes. "Good night." A couple of minutes later her eyes popped open again.

Chapter 3
She's Wearing the Airport Shoes

At breakfast, Julia did her best to not look over. Scott watched with amusement. "We're supposed to get in some tiny boats and paddle up some little backwater streams. You paddle like hell to get up and float back down. You want to do that?"

"Not really," Julia sighed. "To tell the truth, I don't want to paddle up anything. I didn't sleep very soundly last night."

"Okay, we'll walk around the town. I'm sure they have things for lazy people to do, too."

"Watch it, buster."

"I'll bet we can fish off the pier. Do you want to try and catch our dinner? If we caught anything, I bet they'd cook it up for us."

"We had fish last night. I'm having something different tonight."

"Fine. Let's check the itinerary. I'm sure they have stuff to do—other than paddling."

People left the boat and scattered in all directions. Scott and Julia couldn't find an activity they liked, so they wandered off to see the sights.

At lunch, they found a tiny little restaurant that served salads and hamburgers. "Can I get a grilled cheese made with cheddar?" Scott asked.

"Sure," the waiter said. "And for you, Miss?"

Julia blinked. "You got the note. How nice."

"I'm sorry?" The waiter looked confused.

"I'll have a Caesar salad, thank you."

"With anchovies?"

"Yes, please."

Scott leaned in. "I thought fish was out today?"

"Grilled cheese?" Julia said accusingly.

The waiter looked confused. "Would you like anything to drink?"

"Milk," Scott answered.

"A glass of the house red, please."

"Wait! Not milk. I'll have . . . ummm . . . what wine goes well with grilled cheese?"

The waiter shrugged. "A light white wine, or even the house red, I guess."

"Fine, I'll have a Bud Light."

Julia stared at Scott. He tried to hide his amusement, but finally broke. "Okay, okay. Maybe we should be on the wiener cruse."

"You should be, anyway."

"There's a wiener cruise?" the waiter asked. "Do they stop here?"

"Yeah, it does—they do." Scott replied. "And they don't serve Caesar salads on the wiener cruise. So you better stock up."

Julia shook her head at the waiter. "Pay no attention to him. He's just been released from the psychiatric ward."

Their mystery couple wheeled in, the woman got up and walked to a table, while he collapsed the wheelchair and put it by the door.

"You did this on purpose," Scott said, turning the tables on Julia—it was always her line.

Julia was at a loss for a comeback. Finally she admitted, "Okay, I guess I deserved that."

Scott got up saying, "I have to use the men's room." He passed the mystery couple's table on the way to the john. On the way by he suddenly twisted his head around to look at the floor beneath the table and bumped into the wall.

Julia covered her smile with her hand.

He recovered and went to the men's room. He came back in a few minutes looking dead serious.

"Hey there, clumsy," she said.

Scott ignored her. "You were dead right, Jules. There's something very wrong here. Wheelchair lady is wearing the shoes I saw in the airport."

"What? What shoes?"

"When we took off our shoes to go through the body machine—I saw Nelly put those shoes on, after she went through."

"Really?"

"That's why she was trying to be invisible. She's not that guy's wife—she's Nelly."

Julia grabbed her stomach. "Ohhh."

"Well, that explains the splash I heard. And you called it. You really are psychic, Jules."

"No it doesn't," Julia snapped. "No I'm not."

"Whose side are you on? The minute this turns real, you go the other way?"

"No, I didn't mean it that way. I didn't want it to be a murder. I wanted it to be something less sinister—like salmon smuggling or something."

"Salmon smuggling isn't sinister," Scott smiled. "Boy, I bet you couldn't say that fast, three times."

"Please don't try." Julia shook her head. "All of a sudden I'm feeling queasy."

"We need a ship count. We need to find out how many people are supposed to be on board."

"Ohh, here we go." Julia put both hands on her forehead and dropped her elbows on the table.

"We need to get back. I have to see the captain. You want to come along?" Scott was already up. "Okay, lets go."

"No thanks." Julia kept her hands on her head. "I'll catch up to you later."

"Your choice." Scott dashed off.

"We're up the river and he's setting fire to all the paddles. I knew it! I knew we shouldn't have gotten on that boat."

~~~~~~~~~~

Captain Harley Mills was unwilling to let Scott look at the ship's passenger list. "We don't give out that kind of information. If you think you know someone on board, just go look for him or her and say hello. It's a small ship."

"Can you tell me if there's a single on board, at least? A single cabin?"

"All our rooms are double or more. We have suites, but no singles."

"So, no singles?"

"What are you after, Mr. Moss? Is there a problem with your accommodations?"

"No, everything's fine. I just thought I saw someone I knew a little earlier."

"What's the name?"

"I don't know her name. I just thought she kinda looked familiar."

Captain Mills frowned. "And you think she's alone on this cruise?" He leaned forward. "You're not on this vacation alone, are you, Mr. Moss? I believe you're married. Isn't that right? You're here with your wife?"

"Whoa, whoa! I'm not looking for a shipboard hook-up. I'm actually on my honeymoon."

The captain gave Scott a hard stare. Finally, he said, "Have a nice honeymoon, Mr. Moss. And good luck to Mrs. Moss."

Scott backed away with his hands up.

When Scott left, the captain signaled the chief steward. "Ron, keep an eye on that guy. I'm afraid he's going to be trouble."

~~~~~~~~~~

"The captain doesn't like me," Scott said when he got back to their cabin.

"What a surprise. Can we get off the boat at the next stop and take a bus or a car back?" Julia sounded defeated. "I never should have pointed that couple out. Now look at us. We're neck deep in a mystery that you'll never let go of until we know

37

what's going on. And pretty soon everybody on the boat will be mad at you, and we'll have to stay in our cabin just to survive."

"Oh, come on. Its not that bad." Scott gently thumped his head on the wall a couple of times and then just rested his forehead on it.

Julia waited for him to do something else, but he just stood with his head on the wall. "For God sakes, Charley Brown, what should we do? We don't have a shred of evidence that something sinister is going on. And if Nelly, as you call her, has taken the real wife's place, how could we prove it? We don't even know their names."

Scott grabbed his camera and started for the door. "I'll be back."

"Where are you going?"

"I want to take a look at the photo I took of them when they came on board. I'm going to the computer room."

"Hey wait a minute! I'm coming with you. I'm not spending my . . . our honeymoon all alone in this room while you go traipsing off on this misguided adventure on your own."

"Suit yourself. But it's a cabin." And Scott was off like a bullet.

"Dammit!" Julia chased after him.

Scott had to wait five minutes to get on one of the computers. Finally on, he checked the photo on a large computer screen. "Anything jump out at you, Jules?"

"No."

"That's it? Just no?"

"Okay, fine. No, there doesn't seem to be anything in the photograph that would cause me to take notice. Not immediately, anyway. And I find the photo rather . . ."

"Whoa, whoa." Scott held up a hand. "I'll take no for an answer."

". . . boring."

"You had to finish it, didn't you?"

"What would you call it?"

"I would call it a visual record of information that may contribute—somewhere down the line—to an ongoing investigation."

Julia shrugged. "It's still boring."

"Ohh, that's just mean." Scott headed back to their cabin.

Julia followed him in, and sat on the bed. "So, what do we do now?"

"We have to make friends with them."

Julia sat, stunned, for a minute, then they both started laughing a dark, sad little laugh. Julia fell back on the bed, put a pillow over her face, and thrashed her legs like a child. Her muffled scream was barely audible.

Scott shook his head. "Hi, we're the Moses. I'd like to get to know you so I can have you arrested for the murder of your wife."

~~~~~~~~~~

At breakfast Scott and Julia were trying to figure out how to introduce themselves to the mystery couple. "Why don't we just go over and say a nice friendly hello? That's what people from someplace like Ohio would do."

"We're not from *someplace like Ohio*, we're from LA. We don't do that."

"Says you." Scott jumped up and went over to their table. "Hi. I noticed you've been able to get up out of your chair now and then. You seem to be recovering nicely from—whatever."

Jason stared at Scott. "Yes. Recovering from a small case of mind your own damn business." The woman said nothing while the man glared. "Get the hell away from us, okay?"

Scott backed away. "Just trying to be friendly."

When Scott got back to their table, Julia said, "That went well."

"You could tell, huh?" Scott noticed the man talking to the waiter, and then the headwaiter, who got on the phone. "Uh-oh."

"What?"

"Nothing."

"You do realize that now he's going to be watching us as closely as we're watching him."

"If we're right, and we are, he'll be watching us and everybody else pretty close. Until they can get off this boat, that is." Scott paused. "Where do you think they hid the body?"

"In the river, two days back," Julia said, flatly.

"It's a good bet," Scott answered.

"No. I was trying to be funny," Julia said.

"No. Wondering how long she can hold her breath underwater is funny."

Julia's answer was a shudder.

A few minutes later the chief steward came to their table. "Mr. Moss. I afraid I'm going to have to ask you to stop pestering the other passengers. There's been a complaint."

Scott smiled broadly. "That nails it. I need you to take me to the captain right away." Scott got up. "Jules, do you want to come along? I'm going to lay it all out for our captain. You might want to add something."

"We don't have anything yet, Scott," Julia said as she tossed her napkin. "But what the heck, why not start at the top? You can annoy the captain, the vice-captain, and work your way down through the first mate, the second mate, the stewards, and all the way to the cleaning crew."

There is no vice-captain," Scott said, amused.

The chief steward, Ron, looked confused, then said, "Captain Mills is very busy right now, Mr. Moss. We can't just barge in on him."

"I'm sure he is. But is he too busy to hear about a possible murder? If it were my boat, I'd want to be barged in on, wouldn't you?"

"There was no murder." Ron seemed annoyed.

"As John Wayne said in the movie Rio Bravo, 'We'll remember you said that'." Then added, "So later you can explain it to the authorities."

Ron stood frozen for a moment, then sighed and said, "Right this way, Mr. Moss."

"That's the spirit, chief." Scott grinned. "Are you coming, Jules?"

"Do I have a choice?" She got up and quietly said, "This will end badly."

They followed the steward, Julia shaking her head all the way. "I knew I was right. We never should have gotten on this boat."

"Just remember. You started it."

"I started it? What are you, twelve?"

Scott was contrite. "Okay, let's not call this our honeymoon, okay? I'm sorry I let this get out of hand. Let's call this a Murphy. We can write this off, and pick a nice quiet spot for a real honeymoon when we get back. A do-over. What do you say?"

"Why not? If we're still alive when this is over, you've got a deal," Julia answered.

~~~~~~~~~~~

Captain Harley Mills sat back in his chair. "You have something urgent to tell me? I understand it's something about a suspected murder?"

Scott handed the captain his business card. "I'm a private investigator—a trained professional. You have a couple on your riverboat, a man, the one with his wife, fake wife, in a wheelchair, that may have committed murder."

"May have? Fake wife? What the hell are you talking about?" Harley Mills studied the card.

Scott took a deep breath. "A woman came on board with no luggage. Actually she may have snuck on board."

"Sneaked," Julia said.

Scott started to speak, paused, and then turned to Julia. "Sneaked? Really?"

Julia shrugged—Captain Mills glared.

"Anyway, she somehow *sneaked* on board and then disappeared—as far as we can tell. She was a single and you don't have any singles. The man with his wife in a wheelchair came on board late, toward the end of the boarding process, and went directly to their cabin. She looked frail when they boarded, but not so frail the next morning. I have before and after photos of her in the chair. You can see a slight difference. She's about the same height, with the same hairdo, but not as bent over."

Also, her clothes don't fit," Julia added.

"Photos? Clothes? Hairdos? Bent over?" The captain's eyes darted between them. "Just tell me about this murder you witnessed."

"Now it gets tricky," Scott said, "We only heard the splash of the real wife's body hitting the water. It happened at three in the morning, the first night out. We were both up very late, talking, and we both heard it."

Captain Mills looked at Julia. She handed him her card. "I'm a lawyer—an officer of the court."

Harley looked at her card for a moment. "Okay, you're an officer of the court. And?"

"This is all circumstantial, I know. But don't you think it bears looking into?" Julia asked.

"And how would I do that?" Mills asked, looking skeptical. "You heard a splash and you want me to—do what? Drag the river?"

"Not the whole river, just where your boat was the first night out. At three o'clock. You must have a log of where you were at that exact time, right?" Scott looked hopeful.

Julia looked dubious. "He's not going to do that on your say-so, Scott. There's no proof of anything right now. We have to bring the captain proof."

"I'm afraid your wife is right," the captain said. "We check everyone on and off the boat, and the passenger count is correct—so nobody's missing. And I can't have you snooping around, bothering our passengers, Mr. Moss. I'm afraid you'll have to keep your speculations to yourself. Understood? You can't run around bothering the other passengers. Do you understand?"

"Yeah, I understand." Scott studied Mills for a long moment. "So, Captain, how do I get us thrown off your boat?"

The captain was taken aback by the question, but replied, "We stop in the morning as we have every morning, in another quaint little fishing village, Mr. Moss. You can do what you wish when we dock. If you don't come back before we embark, it's not my problem."

"No, I don't think so. I want to get thrown off your boat." Scott smiled. "I want a refund."

The captain didn't skip a beat. "If that's all it takes to get you and your wild accusations out of my hair, I'll be glad to pro-rate a refund."

Scott was already nodding *yes* when Julia took his arm to stop him. "I'm sorry, Captain Mills. That won't be good enough. As a private investigator, Scott intends to pursue this matter until the all facts have been brought out. We'll be staying on your boat until he's uncovered the crime that we believe has been committed."

Harley Mills shot out of his chair with fury in his eyes. "The hell you will! You're off this boat first thing in the morning!"

"That'll be just fine, Captain Mills," Julia said. "We'll be discussing a full refund with your legal representatives, Captain." Julia smiled. "And what arrangements do you have to deliver us safely back to your home port? I expect those expenses will be covered, as well."

While the captain stammered, Scott added, "And I'm pretty sure the local police and television stations will be very interested in your cover-up of a serious crime." He smiled. "Plus, your dumping passengers off—up the river without a paddle. That should be real good for business."

"Really good," Julia quipped.

Scott stabbed his head at Julia. "What she said."

Slightly confused by their repartee, Harley stared them down for a moment, and then picked up his phone. "Please excuse me, I have some business to attend to. I'll see you first thing in the morning, Mr. Moss." He nodded. "Mrs. Moss." He waited until Scott and Julia were out in the passageway and called his corporate legal.

~~~~~~~~~~

The next morning the captain was much calmer. "If there's been a crime on this boat, we'll be very happy to cooperate with the local authorities. I've alerted the police in the next village. They would like to interview you and Mrs. Moss."

"Weston-Moss," Julia interrupted. "This has become a legal matter."

Harley Mills hesitated. "Okay. Mrs. Weston-Moss. The Alaska State Troopers have been informed of your concerns. They . . ."

"It's Mrs. Weston-Moss Holmes, while we're looking into this crime," Scott interrupted.

Captain Mills glared.

"You know, Sherlock Holmes?" Scott paused. "Unimportant detail."

Mills took an irritated breath and continued, "They will have an officer here as soon as possible to interview you as well. In the meantime, if you will please write out a statement explaining what you believe you saw and heard." The captain slid a pad over to Scott. "In as much detail as you can remember. I will see to it that the authorities are given your statement."

Julia smiled. "It sounds like you got the right legal advice, Captain."

"Yes, I did. I'm also advised that you have no legal jurisdiction here, or anywhere for that matter. But we're willing to fully cooperate with you to get to the bottom of this . . . whatever the hell this is." The captain smiled. "I'm sure I didn't say all of that quite right. But I think you get the general idea, Mrs. Weston-Moss."

Scott looked at Julia. "Did he say it right?"

"Yes, he did, Scott," Julia said. She smiled patronizingly as she turned to the captain. "Thank you very much, Captain, for your cooperation. Your legal folks were right on the money."

"In the meantime please keep your snooping to yourselves. The local authorities will board the boat when we dock. After that, you're in their hands."

"Whoa, whoa," Scott stopped writing. "I'm happy to work with the local folk, but murder is a little out of their league, don't you think?"

"You have no proof of a murder, Mr. Moss— only a speculation. In any case, you can deal with the Alaska State Troopers. I'm sure they'll measure up to your LA standards." The captain paused. "By the way, the Los Angeles chief of police asked me to say 'Hello' for him."

"You called them—of course," Scott said.

"Ohh, yes." The captain gave Scott a sideways glance. "You know, they don't like you very much down there. They were overjoyed to hear you were up here in Alaska."

"Terrific," Scott said.

Captain Mills leaned back and smiled. "And I'll be overjoyed when you're back in LA."

"Ouch." Scott continued to write his statement and suddenly stopped. "Hey. Did you ever get your twenty-pound weights back?"

"What weights?"

"In your exercise room. Your twenty-pounders were missing. We heard it over the intercom on the first night out."

Mills looked at the chief steward. The steward nodded. "They weren't returned. So far the cleaning staff hasn't found them in any cabin."

"Wow!" Scott threw up his hands. "Now you gotta drag the river. They weren't just taken off to somebody's cabin. Somebody—and we all know who—used them to weight down a body."

"We don't *gotta* do anything, Mr. Moss. You can take it up with the State Troopers." But now the captain looked worried.

"Thank you, Captain." Julia got up to leave. She waited while Scott scribbled the last sentence of his statement, and said, "We've enjoyed the cuisine."

"Terrific," Harley said.

"We'll tell all our friends," Scott added, as he slid the pad back to the captain.

"Even better," the captain said sarcastically, and then stared at Scott's statement. He continued to stare at it long after they were gone.

The chief steward hesitated. "You look worried, Captain Mills. Do you think it's something we should look into?"

The captain didn't answer right away. Finally he said, "No. Yes. Maybe. Hell, I don't know, Ron. The people in LA don't seem to like him very much, but I could tell they respect him. He's broken some high-profile cases down there." Captain Mills paused. "We'll leave it to the authorities, but I'd like to know exactly where we were at three bells the first night out. Please have Charley mark it on a map for me, will you? I'll want to give it to the State Troopers."

"Yes, sir." Ron headed for navigation.

Chapter 4
The Captain Is a Russian Spy

That evening at dinner, Scott and Julia tried to pretend their mystery couple wasn't there. Scott lasted for about five minutes. "Ahh, this is stupid." Scott tossed his napkin and marched over to their table. "Hey, I'm sorry I bothered you. I just came over to tell you I won't be coming over anymore. So you can enjoy your vacation without a care in the world, okay?"

"You came over here to tell us you won't be coming over here anymore?" The husband glared. "Are you kidding?"

"Yeah well, except for this one last time," Scott said, "I promise—last time."

"Go away."

"Absolutely," Scott said, "And when the police come on board tomorrow, I'll explain that I was probably mistaken when I thought someone was thrown overboard that first night. I just wanted to let you know."

The woman's hands started shaking and she dropped her wine glass.

"Get the hell away from us. You're upsetting my wife." The man was furious.

"Yeah, I'm sorry." Scott looked at her. "You're the new wife, huh?"

Before she could respond, the chief steward came up and muscled Scott away from the table. "We have a brig, you know. It's just a room, but it has a steel door. And if you go anywhere near those two again, you'll be sitting in it until the authorities get here. Do you understand?"

"Sure, whatever you say. But you should know that when I told them the police are coming on board tomorrow, the woman really freaked." Scott glanced back. "And now the man is freaking too."

Ron looked back; the two were in a terrible whispering argument. She was shaking her head and crying. He was squeezing and yanking her hand to get her attention.

"Does that look like a couple with nothing to hide?" Scott asked. "Is that what innocent people do, Ron? Is that an innocent reaction to hearing the cops are coming on board?"

Ron studied them for a moment. He finally said, "Who the hell knows what they're arguing about? It could be anything." Then he sighed. "But you have to stay away from them, okay? I don't know what's going on, but the police will handle the situation in the morning, okay?" Ron let go of Scott's arm. "Sorry about the strong-arm tactics."

Scott smiled. "No offense but, you don't know what strong-arm tactics are, Ron."

The steward looked confused.

50

"Unimportant detail. Look, do me a favor. Keep an eye on them, will you? I promise I'll stay away, but you can't let them disappear before morning, okay? Don't let them vanish, okay?"

"Not a problem, Mr. Moss. They can't get off the boat until we dock."

"Well, don't let them get off in the morning."

"There's no way I can do that. They haven't done anything wrong. And in any case you're not in charge, Mr. Moss, the captain is. And he told me to keep an eye on *you*."

"Okay, fine." Scott gently wagged a finger at him. "But you know I'm right."

"I don't know anything, Mr. Moss," Ron said.

"Yeah, you do." Scott walked away backwards. "You know. And you know I'm right—I can see it in your eyes." He gave Ron a one-finger stab, and went back to his dinner.

Julia waited for him to sit down. "You done?"

"Did you see how they reacted?"

"Yes. What did you tell them? It looked like they were going crazy."

"I told them the police were coming on board in the morning."

Julia was stunned. "Why would you do that?"

"To see their reaction. Innocent people don't react that way," Scott said. "Innocent people look a little confused and then go on eating their dinners."

"But now they know you know. They'll have time to think up a story."

"They already have a story. You don't toss your old wife overboard and have a replacement wife all

51

ready to take her place without thinking it through, right? This is premeditated and well planned."

"Good point." Julia put her napkin on her plate.

Scott paused to think. "Whoa! They have to have planned this well past the riverboat trip. They have to have a plan for when they get back home. They've already figured out how to slip the new wife in without causing any ripples at home, right? Or to be more accurate, roll her in."

"Another good point."

"Damn! This is only the tip of the iceberg."

Julia shook her head. "You had to use that analogy, didn't you?"

"Well, it fit so nicely, I really did. Don't you want coffee or dessert?" Scott asked. "I bet they have a nice Crème Brule."

Julia looked at him incredulously. "*A murder, a fake wife, and a very nice Crème Brule* in the same breath. You're talking about dessert *now*? Like nothing is happening."

"Well, we don't know the Crème Brule is *very nice*. I could be just average nice," Scott said.

Julia got up. "I don't want any dessert. Let's get a brandy in the bar or something. I'm tired of not looking over at them."

"Good girl. Brandy in the bar it is." Scott tossed his napkin and got up.

~~~~~~~~~~

Jason Fellows wheeled his wife up to their cabin. "Don't panic, Joyce. There isn't anything for them to find out. We're a husband and wife on a cruise. Just like everyone else on this boat."

"You said this would be quick and quiet. Now the police are coming. Oh God. They're going to find out and we're going to prison!"

"We're not going anywhere. But, Joyce, you have to keep it together. We're innocent. So start acting like it!"

"How can you say that? He knows!"

"He doesn't know anything. We're husband and wife in this cabin, that's it. There's nothing else to know. But, if you don't calm down they *will* have reason to suspect something."

"I think we should get off the ship first thing in the morning and not come back. We can get a car and drive to the airport and fly back to Denver and no one will be the wiser."

"If we run, they'll know something is wrong. We have to stay here and tough it out."

"I'm not tough!" she screamed. "And I hate that name. Why can't you call me Beverly in private at least? No one can hear us."

"Because we can't afford a slip-up. I have to call you Joyce—it's on our tickets. And you have to react to that name—your name. I'm sorry, but you'll just have to get used to it. At least until we're off this damn boat."

Beverly sat on the edge of the bed and held her head in her hands. "Where are we going to move?"

"I've made it seem like we're moving to Florida, *Joyce.* "I've talked about fishing in the Gulf and hurricanes. But we're actually moving to

53

San Diego. Our Denver house already has a sale pending, and her few friends know we're moving. It shouldn't be more than a week. When we're gone, if any of her old friends try to look her up they'll never find her—you. And if enough time passes they'll stop looking. I've thought this through very carefully, Joyce."

"But what if one of her old friends accidentally sees me? What happens then?"

"You just had a facelift and you look different, that's all. That actress, Jennifer somebody, had one and she looked completely different. So do lots of people. But no one is going to see you."

"How long will I have to be *Joyce*?"

"When I move; I'm going to rent at first. And I'm going to use my middle name. You'll join me, and then you can go back to being Beverly. Everyone in San Diego will know us as William and Beverly Fellows. That's the reason I booked this trip under a false name; so we couldn't be traced. No one at home even knows where we are. They think we're staying in an old rustic cabin in Michigan. I've come back to sign the papers at the closing, while you stayed at the rustic cabin in Michigan. That's what I'll tell anyone who asks. There's no electricity there—I'll say her cell phone battery ran down, so she can't be reached—and her so-called friends never really cared about her, so they won't try to call. Everything's going to work out, Joyce. I've planned this very carefully. I've been thinking this through ever since we met."

"Then why is that man watching us? Why is he suddenly calling the police?"

"Because . . . because he's just some stupid little guy who should be minding his own business. If we have to talk to the police, we'll tell them we don't know what the jerk is talking about, and it'll be over. The police can't just investigate on some wacko's say-so. They have to have some sort of evidence to start an investigation. And there is none. We're just a husband and wife on vacation. There's nothing to investigate."

Beverly didn't look convinced. She went to the cabin window and looked out.

Jason watched her for a moment, and then went to her. He noticed the spectacular rock formations they were just passing. "That's awesome, isn't it?"

"What is?" *Joyce* was staring out the window, but she wasn't seeing anything.

~~~~~~~~~~~

"Hey, Jules, you should see the rocks jutting out of the water and running up the bank, they're really amazing." Scott was looking out their window at the same rocks. "Jules, are you looking? It's really pretty fantastic."

"What? Yes, beautiful," she said, but her mind was elsewhere. She stared, blankly ahead.

Scott watched her for a moment. "Where are you Jules? You look a million miles away."

"Huh? I'm sorry, what?" She came into focus.

"What's on your mind, kiddo?"

"I don't know. You know that couple with the wheelchair was like a black cat running across our honeymoon." Julia sighed and lay back against the pillows. "I know you said we'd have a do-over, but this was supposed to be . . . it. Whatever we do won't be the real honeymoon after this. It'll be . . . I don't know . . . the substitute."

Scott dropped his head. "Dammit."

"What is it that I always say? It's never dull."

Scott was contrite. "I'm sorry about messing up our honeymoon, kiddo. But you know we can't let this go. You know they've done the real wife in and the fake new wife is taking her place."

"Yes, I know. But right now I want it to be dull. I don't want to catch murderers. I want a nice, quiet little respite from the mayhem. For one lousy week I want us to be the couple from Ohio. You're not even getting paid for this . . . business."

"I know, but I can't undo the last three days. It happened, and I'm really sorry."

"Yes, I know." Julia curled up on the bed. "We never should have gotten on this boat."

~~~~~~~~~~

Dallas Bunch of the Alaska State Troopers was waiting at the dock when the riverboat made port. Scott and Julia met with him in the captain's quarters. After Scott told his story in great detail, Officer Bunch rubbed his face, took a breath and said, "Okay. So this woman, who's in a wheelchair, was wearing the same pair of shoes as some other woman—who doesn't seem to be anywhere on the boat—and there are two twenty-pound weights missing from the exercise room. And you heard a splash." Dallas stared at his meager notes. "That's it? That's your evidence of a murder?"

"Well, when you say it like that, it doesn't sound so airtight," Scott answered.

"Look, Mr. Moss, while two women wearing the same shoes might upset the fashion police, it doesn't rise to the level of criminal activity. And the theft of exercise weights is petty theft at best." Dallas closed his little notebook. "It took me three hours to get here this morning to hear *this*?"

"Ask Ron, here. He saw them react."

"Go ahead." Officer Bunch turned and waited for Ron to say something.

Ron hesitated for a moment, then finally said, "When the couple in question heard you were coming on board they seemed a little upset."

"So was I!" Bunch exclaimed, "When I found out very late last night that I had to drive all the way up here this morning."

"Well, it seemed a *little* suspicious, I guess." Ron said. "I saw them arguing a little afterward, but it could have been about anything."

"Arguing a little!" Scott exclaimed. "Nobody innocent acts that way."

Bunch thumped his book. "Look, all I can do is talk to them, and only if they will let me. With what little you've told me, and with no hard evidence, I can't force them to do or say anything. If they don't want to talk to me, they don't have to. I can't make them talk to me without probable cause." Dallas sighed, "They have the right to be left alone."

"He's right," Julia said.

"Gee, thanks, Jules," Scott quipped.

Julia said, "Glad to help," with half a smile.

The captain interjected, "Look, Officer Bunch, I don't know what kind of people they are, but if you bother them in any serious way, I could be looking at a lawsuit."

"For just talking?" Scott wasn't buying it.

"He's right, Scott," Julia said.

"Again. Thanks, Jules," Scott grumbled.

"Yes, I know, Captain." Bunch huffed out a deep breath. "So would the Alaska State Troopers."

Captain Mills gave Officer Bunch the river map. "Here's where we were at the time Mr. Moss said they heard the splash. It was three in the morning. It doesn't sound like you'll need it but—just in case."

"Okay." Bunch took the map. "Look, I can't just wander up to them at breakfast and interrogate them. It would brand them for the rest of the trip. The rest of the passengers would probably treat them differently and it would ruin their vacation. I'd like to speak with them in private to avoid any embarrassment—and any lawsuits."

"I can have Ron ask them to meet with you in the card room. No one ever goes in there in the morning," the captain said.

"Fine. Right after breakfast, then. But this is a simple request. They can't be forced to come talk to

58

me if they don't want to." Bunch abruptly got up. "Where's the card room?"

"I'll show you," Ron said, and led him down the deck. "Would you like some coffee? I can have a pot brought in. It might make the interview seem a little less official."

"Don't kid yourself," Bunch said. "Any time you get summoned by the police, informal or not, it's official. But coffee would be great, thanks." He sounded exhausted. "Believe it or not, the roads are very busy at three in the morning. They're full of fishermen who aren't in any big hurry. And even empty, the trip up those two-lane roads isn't easy."

Ron pointed through the door. "Right in there, Officer Bunch. I'll talk to them, and bring in some coffee." And he was off.

~~~~~~~~~~

Jason Fellows—traveling under the name of Mr. Jerald Butane—marched into the card room, furious. "What the hell is this all about? That lunatic told me yesterday you were coming on board. Don't tell me you actually listened to his rambling nonsense?"

"I'm sorry, Mr. Butane," Bunch said, "This will only take a minute."

"You're damn right it will," Jason growled, "I'm a lawyer. You've got one minute, and then I'm going back to my wife."

"Would you like some coffee?" Dallas asked.

"You have one minute, Officer!" Jason barked.

Officer Bunch rubbed his face. "I'm sorry, Mr. Butane. A Mr. Moss thinks something happened on board the first night out. I'm just here to follow it up. I'm sure you can understand."

"Not really, no."

"Well please try to understand, Mr. Butane. I have to follow this up."

"Really?" Butane stared him down. "Well, I think the captain is a Russian spy. Would you like to follow *that* up, please?"

"Mr. Butane, please," Bunch pleaded.

"I don't have any facts, I know, but I'd like you to search his quarters anyway." Fellows pointed at the captain. "He might have some secret documents hidden in his desk. I'm going to have to insist you take his desk apart. Board by board."

Bunch closed his little book. "I'm sorry to have bothered you, Mr. Butane. This has been a very big misunderstanding. Thank you for your time."

Fellows turned for the door. "And if that little jerk comes within ten feet of me or my wife, you'll have the biggest lawsuit you've ever seen on your hands, Captain. Goodbye."

The captain waited for man he knew as Butane to storm out before turning to Officer Bunch. "You can bill Mr. Moss for your time and travel. Isn't that how false alarms are handled?"

"Hmmm." Bunch sat, tapping his little book on the table. "Not usually the first time. The public has the right to make a few mistakes. We usually wait for a second or third one." He continued to tap his notebook, thinking. Finally he stood up. "Well, thank you, Captain."

"That's it?"

"For now. Let me know if anything more comes up." He handed the captain a card. "You can reach me at this number."

Captain Mills took the card. "You mean, if anything floats to the surface."

They both had that look—that something wasn't quite right—that Scott might be correct.

"Especially if anything floats to the surface." Officer Dallas Bunch left rubbing his forehead.

Captain Mills put Bunch's card with the two business cards from Julia and Scott and suddenly stopped. "Everybody has a card these days. Cops, private investigators, lawyers . . . most lawyers." He paused. "Actually all lawyers." He stared at the three cards for a moment and then the door. "Hmmm?"

The captain turned to Ron. "You know what? Why don't you take shore leave today, Ron? Wander around, see the sights, sort of watch over things. Make sure our passengers are happy. Make sure everything stays . . . normal."

Ron smiled. "You got it Captain. I'll keep an eye out for trouble."

Ron left and Captain Harley Mills fiddled with the three business cards.

Chapter 5
Save the Whales

As the passengers left the ship that morning, Scott and Julia made sure they went in the opposite direction as Mr. Butane and his wife.

When Ron wandered off the boat in street clothes he looked like just another passenger. Except that he didn't know who to follow—Mr. and Mrs. Moss, or Mr. and Mrs. Butane. He stood, blocking the gangway until the man behind him said, "You wanna get off, sonny? It's just dry land. You won't get seasick or anything."

"Oh. Sorry about that." Ron quickly moved out of the way. He shrugged and went in the direction Mr. Butane had wheeled his wife.

As they had in the past, Joyce rode for a while and then walked for a little. Other passengers worked their way down the same streets, buying trinkets, clothing, and food.

Ron noticed the same thing Scott had noticed—they went into stores but they didn't buy anything, they looked at very little, and they paid for lunch with cash. It was very obvious that they were killing time more than anything else. "Ah, dammit to hell," Ron mumbled.

He followed them into a little gift shop, hesitated, and finally went up, stood next to them, looked the other way, and said, "You have to buy a couple crappy souvenirs now and then, Jason. You have to act like everybody else."

"It's Jerald, you dumb jackass. And we're not supposed to know each other."

Ron continued looking away but kept talking. "Fine, *Jerald*. But you two have to blend in better." He noticed that other passengers were in the store. "My ass is on the line just as much as yours."

Joyce's hands started shaking. "Oh, God."

"Relax, Joyce. Everything's fine," Jerald said, as he spun the postcard rack. "What did they say after I left?" he asked, thumbing through the cards.

"Everything's not fine," Joyce mumbled.

Ron bent over and rifled through the bin of stuffed walruses. "They're uneasy. But they're not going to do anything. Just stay the hell away from Moss, and I'll keep an eye on him. And start acting like a tourist, dammit."

"Fine. I'll buy some crap. Happy?"

"Not really. This could very easily get out of hand. I'm not going to prison over this—you got that? You're not paying me enough to spend half my life behind bars." Ron looked around the store, said, "Nice to see you, Mr. Butane—Mrs. Butane," and left the store.

Mrs. Butane quickly got in her wheelchair, put her head in her hands, and started gasping for air.

Mr. Butane grabbed some stuffed animals and laid them on the counter. "We'll take these."

"Oh, you have some young ones back home?" the clerk asked.

"Yeah, dozens. Just put them in a bag, please. We're in a hurry."

The clerk flinched at his manner and rang up the sale. "Fifty-eight thirty. Cash or charge?"

Mr. Butane gave him three twenties, and tossed the bag in Joyce's lap.

She hugged the bag, and he wheeled her out.

"You forgot your change, sir," the clerk called.

But they were gone.

"They won't be back," Scott's voice came out of the shadows. He'd been watching from the back of the store.

"Oh? Do you know them? You can give him the dollar and seventy cents."

"No, they're not going to want it." Scott pointed to the slotted container on the counter, "You can use it to save the whales, or . . . the tuna. Or whatever other fish you're trying to save."

"It's for the herring. They're being over-fished." The clerk pointed to the sign on the can. "They're an important part of the ocean food chain. It's a very serious problem."

"Yeah, I'm sure it is, but I'm more interested in the red herring."

"I'm sorry? Are the red herring dwindling too? I've never heard of that species."

Scott chuckled. "Yeah well, right now there's only one that I know of."

"Only one!"

"Yeah, pro-creation's going to be a bitch." He stuck a five-dollar bill in the can. "Never mind. It was an imperfect metaphor." Scott stared out the shop window, watching Jason maneuver the wheelchair down the street. He looked up and down to make sure Ron wasn't anywhere nearby. "Very interesting." He slipped out a moment later.

The clerk saw the five laying on top of the dimes and quarters and yelled, "Hey! Thanks, a lot Mister! We need more tourists like you."

"Not really." Scott waved at him through the window and headed back to Julia.

~~~~~~~~~~

"Where did you go?" Julia asked when he slipped in behind her. "One minute you were right here and the next minute you were gone. I looked all over for you."

"There's been a very interesting development, Jules." Scott smiled. "The chief steward seems to know our killer."

"Of course! Where else would you go? And why would I even ask?" Julia shook her head.

"Mr. Wheelchair and Ron had a thinly disguised conversation in a gift shop a couple of blocks from here," Scott said. "Ron has to be how the new Mrs. Wheelchair got on board without being noticed."

"Thinly disguised?"

"Ron was talking to a barrel of fish, while Mr. Wheelchair had his back turned to him, having a lively conversation with a big rack of pop-up post cards. Ron's in on it."

"So, what do we do next?" Julia asked.

"We may have to split up."

"Some honeymoon."

Scott smiled. "I'll figure it out. Meanwhile, let's get something to eat. We can decide who follows who, over lunch."

"Whom," Julia corrected.

"Whom? Really?"

"Who follows whom, is correct."

"Whom makes up these rules?"

"Webster. And it's *who* makes up these rules."

"Webster wasn't so much a grammarian as he was a recorder of accepted grammar, wasn't he?"

"Aren't you the smart one."

"That's for others to say," he said with a smile.

"It wasn't a question."

"What was it, then?"

"Webster's dictionary would call it sarcasm."

"I never liked him."

"Who? Mr. Wheelchair?"

"Mr. Webster."

"He's always spoken highly of you."

As they walked down the street looking for an inviting restaurant Scott said, "Ron is just behind us, a half-block back."

"You can see him?" Julia didn't turn around.

"Thanks for not looking. Every once in a while I catch a quick glimpse of him reflected in the windows across the street. He's tailing us."

"But not very well if you saw him."

"Actually, he's pretty good for an amateur. If I hadn't seen him talking to Mr. Wheelchair, earlier, I probably never would have noticed him."

Julia saw a sushi shop. "Oh, look, Scott. Sushi. Do you feel like a little raw fish?"

"Do I *look* like a little raw fish?"

"I walked right into that, didn't I?" Julia paused and then entered the restaurant.

Scott followed her in. "This could be a really big problem for me, Jules."

"How so?"

"What if the sushi here is better than Mas's?"

"What if it rains gumdrops?"

"I can't fly up here every time I want sushi."

"You got that right. We're not coming up here ever again." Julia's voice left no room for doubt.

"Ouch." They found a table and sat down.

As they read the menu, Ron tried to slip by the windows. "Hey, Ron!" Scott bellowed, and the startled man at the next table flipped his piece of sushi a foot into the air. "In here!"

Caught, Ron reluctantly went inside. "Hello Mr. and Mrs. Moss. How are you enjoying the day?"

"The normal way." Scott shoved out a chair with his foot. "Join us."

"Ahhh." Ron wavered. "I better not. I'm not that big on raw fish." He paused. "And we shouldn't really fraternize with our passengers too much."

"Ohhh, that's too bad. Mr. Wheelchair will be sorry to hear that."

"Who?"

"Come on, Ron. You know who I mean."

"Of course he does," Julia said as she opened her napkin. "You're not dumb, are you, Ron?"

"I beg your pardon? I have no idea what you're talking about."

Scott pointed up the street. "You were talking him into buying a bunch of stuffed animals in that gift shop just a few minutes ago."

Ron's face grew pale. He stood for a moment and said, "And now I'm talking to you. We're a friendly crew." He hesitated. "But I have to go."

As they watched Ron leave, Julia said, "You're not leaving yourself much wiggle-room, Scott. If you tip off everyone your job gets harder."

"Yeah, I know." Scott watched, through the window, as Ron left. "But Captain Mills is not on board, the State Troopers are not on board, and Ron's obviously not on board. I'm just trying to shake things up." Scott stood up.

"Are we going back on board ourselves? I thought we were going to have some lunch."

"Very punny. "Maybe somebody will panic and spill the beans."

"Maybe it'll . . ."

"Don't say it." Scott raised a warning finger. "I just want to see where he goes. If he goes to Mr. Wheelchair, that's probably everyone involved. If he hightails it back to the boat, there may be more fish in the stew."

"Third worst mixed-metaphor ever." Julia got up and tossed her napkin.

"Third?"

"Zip it."

They watched Ron wander around the town for a while. "Well, he's not headed back to the ship, he's looking for Mr. Wheelchair. I guess it's just the three of them," Scott said.

"What now, Sherlock?" Julia asked.

"No, you're Sherlock. I'm . . ?" Scott couldn't decide who he was.

"You're not the bumbling Doctor Watson, are you?" Julia paused. "Although, it is surprising how you manage to solve so many cases, considering the ad-lib way you go about it."

"I never claimed to be a planner. In any case, I'm not the Nigel Bruce 'Watson'. They portrayed him smarter and less of a bumbler in later movies. I can live with the newer 'Watson'. Besides, I like being your sidekick for a change. Let's get to the boat." Scott started walking very fast.

Julia grabbed his arm. "Slow down, Watson. They're not going to do anything at this point. The crime's been committed. They just have to wait until they can get off the boat and it's over."

Scott stopped cold. "You're right. We have to find the body before they disappear. Ron will be easy to find, but I'll bet Mr. and Mrs. Wheelchair used false names to book the cruise. And as far as I can tell, they've paid for everything with cash. He's not leaving any kind of paper trail."

"So, here we go." Julia paused. "And by that I mean where *do* we go?"

"Have you ever gone scuba diving?"

"Actually, I have. We used to dive when I was a kid. Our whole family used to dive off Catalina."

"Something else I didn't know. The teenager in the basement and now this Catalina scuba business. What else don't I know about you?"

"There's no teenager. And there's nothing else. I know how to scuba dive, and that's all."

"Good. You can teach me."

"No way, Scott. You'll have to find a certified dive instructor. I'm not going to be responsible for you drowning on our honeymoon."

"No, no. You get a Murphy on the honeymoon. The honeymoon's a do-over. Let's get our stuff and rent a car back to where they dumped the body." Scott was off at a march.

"Lead on, Watson." Julia tried to keep up. "But at a normal pace."

"This is normal," he said, but he was actually speed walking.

"With you nothing is normal. Slow down!"

Scott eased off on his pace. "Fine."

They were back on board the boat, and packed within the hour.

Captain Mills watched Scott and Julia carry their suitcases down the gangway. He fiddled with the three business cards, filing through them one at a time. Finally he called Officer Bunch. "Yeah, Officer Bunch, this is Captain Mills. Mr. Moss and his wife are leaving the boat. I'm not sure what they're going to do, but they'll probably go down river to our homeport" Mills continued to fiddle with the cards. "Or maybe they'll stop where we

71

passed at three bells on the first night out. I thought you should know. You have the map, right? Yeah. I'll keep you informed about anything new on the boat. Thanks." Mills hung up but kept his hand on the phone. "He had to get on *my* ship."

Chapter 6
Nightmares Forever

"You want a room?" the grumpy clerk asked.

"We'd like to rent a car." Scott and Julia were at a small hotel just off the pier.

"So would I," the clerk said, "My truck's been in the shop for a week. Uncle Lloyd can't get parts up here for three more days."

"But there's a car rental place, right?"

"Yeah, somewhere." The clerk didn't offer any more information.

Scott was ready to pull him over the counter and adjust his attitude, when Julia took his arm and said, "We can rent a helicopter, Scott." She was already on her iPhone. "We want to go to the river cruise stops above Juneau. I don't know. It's where they all stop. Yes, the first stop. We're at the fourth stop, wherever that is. You know it—good. No—just one way—two people, two bags—can you tell me how much?" She waited a few moments. "Ouch. Hold on." She covered the phone. "Almost five hundred. What do you think?"

"Fine." Scott didn't look happy.

"Fine, yes. The name on the card is Scott Moss. Where do we meet you?"

"We're using my credit card?" Scott yelped. "I thought this was your case."

Julia waved him off. "One hour. Thank you." She grabbed her suitcase, smiled at the clerk, and said, "Thanks for being such a helpful clerk."

"My dad owns this place. I'm just a clerk now, but I'll be running it some day."

"Yeah, running it into the ground," Scott said to himself, as he followed Julia out.

Two hours later they were hovering over the first stop above Juneau. "Are you sure you want me to set down here? It's a pretty small place."

"Yes. Just find an empty field or parking lot as close to the river as possible, thanks," Scott said.

The pilot set down in an empty lot. Most of the townspeople watched Scott and Julia climb out and duck under the blades. They dragged their suitcases to the road, while two scruffy old men watched with amusement.

Scott nodded. "Hi. Sorry about the noise."

The chopper was off immediately.

"Pretty fancy entrance. You people somethin' special?" one of the old geezers asked.

His gnarly sidekick gave a wolf whistle.

"No. My wife's just afraid of boats," Scott said.

The old guy got it and laughed. The sidekick wore an amused grin.

"Is there a scuba rental place nearby?"

"Scuba? You can't dive in the river. It's way too cold this time of year and the current's super dangerous," the old guy said. "Only crazy Earl does stuff like that."

The old guy's sidekick nodded in agreement. "Crazy Earl's crazy."

"Can you tell us where we can find this crazy Earl?" Julia asked.

"Lives in the house painted red on one side and yellow on the other," the old guy said.

"That part weren't crazy. He jus up an run out of paint," his sidekick added. "The runnin' out of paint was just stupid." Then spit and chuckled.

"Just up the road." The old guy pointed.

"Thanks."

"Is there a place we can stay for a couple of nights?" Scott asked.

"Millie's Bed 'n Breakfast," the old guy said.

"Best biscuits," his sidekick added.

"So . . . Millie and her biscuits would be where, exactly?" Julia asked.

"Just up the road." The old guy pointed again.

"Which road?"

"Only one road," his sidekick said with a grin.

"Thanks." Scott adjusted his photo bag, grabbed both suitcases, and started up the road.

Julia followed, amused by Scott's bravado.

They came to Millie's Bed 'n Breakfast first. "Good. I didn't want to carry these suitcases much further," Scott said.

"You couldn't let those old codgers see me carry my own bag, huh?"

Scott twitched. "You got me. I didn't want those old guys to think . . ."

"Don't get me wrong. I loved it," Julia said. "Maybe those two could follow us around."

"Hey, I do chivalry stuff."

"Mmmm." Julia wiggle-waggled her hand.

"I helped you into the helicopter."

"Right." Julia sarcastically acknowledged.

Scott checked the sun. "Let's get a room and find crazy Earl. We might get a dive in before it gets too dark to see."

"We?"

"You and crazy Earl, okay?"

Julia shook her head. "Never should have gotten on that boat."

They checked into Millie's B and B, and easily found the two-tone house a hundred yards up the road. Scott knocked on the door. They heard a little rustle and then silence for over a minute. "Earl?" He knocked again and sniffed the air. "What's that funny smell?"

"You know darn well what that *funny* smell is. We're dealing with a pothead."

The curtains moved a little.

"We're not cops, Earl!" Scott shouted. "We have a business proposition for you."

They waited, still no movement inside.

"Come on, Earl! We're willing to pay for your services," Julia said.

"What kind of services?" a voice yelled from somewhere out behind the house.

"We need your expertise." Scott yelled back.

"I'm no expert at anything." Earl peeked out from behind his house. "And I'm all sold out."

Julia stared at Scott. "Ohh, wonderful."

"We don't want your weed, Earl. We want to go scuba diving," Scott said.

"Really?" Earl walked, unsteadily, from behind his little red and yellow house. He was clearly high. "Water's pretty cold. You gotta wear a heavy-duty winter wetsuit."

"Yes, really. And a wetsuit is fine." Julia said, "We'd like to get a dive in this afternoon. Do you have a suit my size?"

Earl sized her up. " I got one close enough. But no can do. I'm too stoned." Earl could barely stand. "Morning's better anyway."

"You'll be un-stoned by then?" Scott asked.

"Depends. How much?"

"A hundred bucks."

"Deal!" Crazy Earl almost fell over backwards smacking his hands together. "Sun's up at six. I'll be here." Earl stumbled back up on his porch and grabbed the doorknob. It was locked. "Oops." He knocked on the door and stood there, weaving.

"It's your house, Earl," Scott said.

"Ohh, right." Earl went around back.

Scott turned to Julia. "I don't know, Jules. Are you sure you want to go diving with him?

"I'm not worried about myself. The currents around Catalina were very strong. I learned how to handle it. But once we're in the water, he's on his own." Julia shrugged. "Let's see what he's like in the morning. We can decide then. If he hasn't sobered up, this could end badly," she shook her head. "Very badly."

"No argument there. But we don't have a lot of choices." Scott pointed back down the road. "Let's get some dinner. There has to be at least one diner somewhere in this town."

~~~~~~~~~~~

They were up at five, devouring eggs and really great biscuits with sausage-laced cream gravy. A short while later, they were back at crazy Earl's. "Here goes nothing." Scott gently knocked on the door. "Let's hope he's straightened up enough to keep from drowning."

When Earl opened the door he was all business. "The gear is in the shed out back, by my boat. You got the money?"

"Yeah, I ha . . ."

"Good. You can pay me after the dive." Sober, Earl was a different man. "Do you have anything in mind when we go? Or just a scary look-see at fish swimming in the current? There are spots that stay quite calm. That's the best place to watch the fish. But, I have to warn you, the salmon aren't running up the river yet—at least I haven't seen any. It's still a tad early, I guess."

"Actually, what we're looking for is . . . a fairly large item about the size of a person." Scott waited to gauge Earl's reaction. "We're guessing it's probably light colored, and weighted down."

Earl looked past Scott and Julia, up the road. "Ahhh. No shit. You gotta be kidding."

"No. It's a little hard to explain."

"Don't bother. The State Troopers will probably explain it better." Earl pointed, as Officer Bunch pulled into Earl's yard and got out of his car.

"Didn't see that coming," Scott whispered.

"Hello, Officer Bunch," Julia called out. "What brings you here so early in the morning?"

Bunch didn't bother with pleasantries. "I have the map with the exact location you were passing, at three in the morning. If we find a body, the state will pay any fees." He turned to Earl. "We're using your boat, correct?"

"Yeah. My name's Earl. I'm a certified diver. They didn't tell me much. What's going on?"

"Mr. and Mrs. Moss think there may be a woman's body down there—weighted down with forty pounds of barbells. Do you think you can find that spot, Earl?"

Earl studied the map. "Yeah, I know it. Been there dozens of times."

Scott said, "Thanks for being so . . ."

"Save it, Moss. I'm really tired," Bunch interrupted. "And I really hope you're wrong, but I can't *not* check your story out. That Mr. Butane didn't seem quite right to me, either, Moss. So what do you say get started?"

Earl had his bearings. "If this is the exact spot, a body thrown overboard, even with weights, would probably have been pushed along the bottom. It would bump along to these little coves before it could settle. The river is real fast right there, but the current softens out in this wider area. That's where I'd start looking. But it's your call, Officer."

"No, it's your call—you know the river. Let's get going." Officer Bunch headed for Earl's boat.

"So, Mr. Wheelchair is Mr. Butane? Cool."

"Cool, Scott? Don't you mean hot?"

"I was being ironic. Butane is cold as a liquid."

"Everybody knows that," Julia said.

"Well, did you know . . ."

Julia slapped her hand over Scott's mouth to stop him. "Don't."

Everyone piled into Earl's boat and Earl headed upriver. "It's clear enough to see the bottom in most of the coves. We should try that first. Can anybody drive a boat?"

"I can," Julia said.

"Good." Earl instantly abandoned the wheel and went to put on his gear. The boat started a gentle turn toward the shore.

"Whoa!" Julia grabbed the wheel to keep the boat from running into the bank. "Wait a minute, Earl. I'm diving, with you."

"That's okay. I can drive it, Mrs. Moss." Officer Bunch took the wheel.

Julia slipped off her jeans and shirt to reveal a stunning black one-piece bathing suit, a deep V neck, squared at the bottom, plunging almost to her waist. She had put it on in the bathroom so Scott wouldn't see it. She gauged his reaction and smiled.

Time stood still for about two seconds for the three men. Earl gulped, Bunch ripped his eyes back to the river, and Scott whispered, "Whoa."

"First place is to look just around that next bend." Earl rescued the moment.

"I had planned on wearing this while lounging around a resort pool," Julia whispered. "Not diving in some ice-cold Alaskan river."

"Yeah, well . . . let me catch my breath and help you suit up." Scott held open the legs of the wetsuit Earl had provided. As she stepped in, the cut of her bathing suit's cleavage was directly at his nose.

Scott's eyes bugged out.

Julia rolled hers. "Yeah. Like you haven't been there before," she whispered.

"And you still got it, kid," he whispered back.

"Damn right."

Earl was paralyzed for another moment, but blinked, and then went on suiting up.

By the time they were over the area, Earl and Julia were in their gear. Everyone peered into the water as Officer Bunch slowly cruised back and forth across the coves. "See anything?"

"Not yet."

"Try over there." Earl pointed.

"What's that?" Scott stabbed a finger into the water. "It looks different from the bottom."

Bunch throttled back and held the boat steady over the spot.

Earl and Julia both rolled off the boat backward. They swam to the bottom. Earl waved no and they came back up. "Just an odd colored rock," Earl said. "Let's try a little further up."

Another dive and another empty bottom. "The current sometimes pushes things to the far side.

81

Why don't we try over there?" Earl pointed, and Bunch pushed the boat to the other bank.

Julia and Earl went over the side. Scott paced the deck. "I hope they find her," he said.

"I hope they don't. I hope you're wrong, Moss," Officer Bunch said. "It's nothing personal."

"Not a problem." Scott peered into the dark, freezing cold water. After a while he checked his watch. "They've been down a long time this time. Do you think everything's okay, Dallas?"

"Earl seems to know the river pretty well, and your Mrs. Moss seems to know what she's doing. I'm sure they're fine, Scott."

Julia popped up thirty yards down river and waved. "Thank God," Scott said. "I was worried,"

Bunch powered over. Two coves and three long dives later, they still hadn't found anything.

"We're out of air," Earl said as he popped up, "We'll have to come back tomorrow."

The ride back was silent. Julia lay out on a seat, exhausted, and closed her eyes. Scott watched her with more than a little concern.

Officer Bunch radioed that he would be another day on the river.

Earl worked on his gear. Scott and Julia went to Millie's B and B. And Dallas seemed to disappear.

Julia rested for an hour, got dressed, and they went out to dinner.

~~~~~~~~~~~

In the morning, Officer Bunch met with Scott and Julia for eggs and biscuits. An extra place was already set for him.

Millie clearly knew Officer Dallas Bunch. She gave him an extra biscuit with extra gravy, and he gave her a little wink.

Scott gave Julia a look, tilted his head in their direction, and raised his eyebrows.

Julia's response was a little smile and a slight downward nod. She thought so, too.

Breakfast over, they found Earl on his boat, in his wetsuit, and all ready to go. "Good morning, everybody. I hope you all had a good night's sleep. I slept like a baby."

"I woke up stiff all over," Julia moaned.

"All set?" Bunch asked.

"You bet. I got extra tanks. Just in case." Earl smacked one of the tanks.

"Hit it." Scott pointed upriver.

Julia started putting on her wetsuit and gear. Scott tried to help her again, but she gently held him at bay. "No, I've got this."

As they went upriver, Scott asked, "So you're not married, Officer Bunch?"

"Nope," Dallas said. "Do I look married?"

"Nope!" Scott said and grinned.

Dallas gave him a stare that turned into a smile, and then a raised eyebrow. "That's none of your concern, Mr. Moss."

Scott held both palms vertical, they both knew what he was implying.

The search went on for two hours before anything showed up on the bottom that looked worth exploring. The first dive found a cream-colored car fender. The second dive found a waterlogged buoy. Nearer the swift current it was harder to see, and harder to swim. Earl and Julia would dive down, coast downriver for twenty yards and come back up.

"Lets take a break," Earl finally said.

Millie had made sandwiches for lunch. Julia really needed the break. Officer Bunch continued to cruise the boat back and forth, and he and Scott peered into the water while they ate.

Two more dives and Julia looked very tired. "It's been a long time since I did this. I don't think I have too many more dives in me."

"What's that?" Bunch pointed to a light V shape on the bottom, just at the head of the cove.

Earl was over in a flash.

Julia pulled her mask down from her forehead.

"Jules don't! Wait!" Scott yelled. But Julia had it on and was back in the water right behind Earl. "Dammit, Jules."

Bunch and Moss watched from above. They could see pretty well in that part of the river. Earl got there first and tried to stop Julia from getting too close. But Julia was already there. Her strong strokes suddenly faltered and she went limp. Her body started to drift with the current.

"Oh, shit!" Scott was in the water headfirst, in his clothes. He swam long, hard, powerful strokes, to get to her.

By the time he got near, Earl had Julia by the arm and had her headed for the surface. Scott met them partway back, and Earl shoved his respirator in Scott's mouth. Scott took a gulp of air and they brought Julia up. She was swimming again by the time they hit the surface. "Are you crazy!" Earl yelled, "The water's thirty-three degrees!"

Scott was shaking too hard to respond. His teeth were chattering and his fingers were already blue. He helped Earl and Officer Bunch get Julia into the boat and tried to get out of the freezing water by himself. His strength sapped, Bunch and Earl had to help him up over the rail. Once in, he started shaking uncontrollably. "Hhhholy ddddamn that's frrrricking cccoldd."

Earl dropped the anchor and Dallas Bunch looked for something to wrap around Scott.

"There's a blanket in the cabin down below," Earl said. He pointed, and Dallas went for it. "I get cold too, sometimes. Even in a zero wetsuit." Earl looked at the shivering Scott and shook his head. "Jeez, they say I'm crazy, but you got me beat by ten miles, brother."

Once wrapped, Scott looked at Julia. She was sitting at the side, drained. "Are you okkkay?" he asked still chattering, "Whattt happeneddd?"

Before Julia could respond, Earl said, "There's a woman's body hung up on the rocks. The current has her pinned, and she's face up, eyes open, mouth open, looking at us. It shocked the hell out of me."

"I'm going to be sick," Julia said, turned, and puked into the water.

An entire school of small fish appeared out of nowhere and gobbled up Millie's pre-digested ham and cheese sandwich. Julia watched for a moment, then laughed and cried at the same time.

"I've seen them do that before." Earl nodded.

Scott went to her, and she buried her head in his chest. "It was awful. She was staring right at me."

"Easy, kid. It's going to be all right." Scott held her and gently rocked her.

"The hell it is. You didn't see her eyes. And she had no teeth—her mouth was just a black hole." Julia gulped. "And a tiny fish swam out of it." She shivered and covered her face with her hands. "Oh God, I'm going to have nightmares forever."

"Try not to think about it, Jules."

"Yeah, right." Julia's sarcastic tone left no room for an argument.

Scott looked at Bunch and shook his head.

Officer Bunch had been on the radio. "A police boat and a rescue boat are on the way. They move pretty fast—it shouldn't be too long."

Officer Bunch called Captain Mills next, but the passengers were already leaving the cruise. "Well, don't let the cleaning people touch their cabin," Bunch said. "We'll want their fingerprints and anything else they may have left behind."

"It may be too late," Mills said. "We have a turn-around time of four hours. We start cleaning the cabins immediately, and the Butanes were the first ones off. It could be finished by now."

"Well, tell them to stop cleaning the room immediately! They might not get everything Mr. or

86

Mrs. Butane touched. We may have to consider it a crime scene."

"Okay, you got it." Harley Mills looked around the boat for Ron, but Chief Steward Ron seemed to have disappeared. "Where the hell did he go?"

By the time Captain Mills got to the Butane cabin, the cleaning crew had moved on. "Damn!"

~~~~~~~~~~

Earl stayed anchored over the body until the rescue boats arrived. It took them two hours to get there. By then Scott had fully recovered, and Julia had collected herself. They sat, sipping coffee and watching, while the police divers did their job.

After they got the body up and covered, the divers went back down.

"What are they doing, now," Julia asked.

"They're looking for her teeth," Bunch said.

"Ohh God." Julia shuddered all over again, fell sideways, and buried herself in Scott's lap.

"They might not even be down there," Scott said. "He's good—really good. No teeth, no identity after the body decomposed. But he didn't plan on us."

"They won't find them in this current, it moves way too fast," Earl said. "If they're there they could be two miles downriver by now." He started the engine. "There's nothing more we can do here. We might as well get out of their way."

As he weighed anchor, Dallas Bunch transferred over to the police boat. "Mr. and Mrs. Moss. I'll need your statements again," he called. "Stay at Millie's until I get back, okay?"

Scott didn't answer.

"We're not staying here, are we?" Julia asked, still lying in Scott's lap. But she already knew what the answer would be.

"We don't have anything to add. But, if they came on board the boat as Mr. and Mrs. Butane, their airline tickets back to wherever may have the same name. We need to get to the Juneau airport."

"Even though it's a different missus, now." Julia sat up. "Officer Bunch!" she called.

"What?" he answered.

"The Juneau Airport. They may have used Mr. and Mrs. Butane on the tickets," she yelled.

"I'll call ahead," Dallas answered.

"Jules!" Scott whined.

"Hey, Mr. do-it-yourself, whether you like it or not, you need the help."

"I thought this was your case?"

"Fine! *I* need the help."

"As long as we're clear on that," Scott smiled.

"We both almost drowned and you're already making jokes?"

"I would never let you drown, Mrs. Moss. Who would make my breakfast?"

"You make your own damn breakfast," she snapped. Then quietly said, "I do the dinners."

Scott flinched. "Who knew marriage would be so orderly? And angry?"

"Zip it." Julia was on the phone. "Hi, it's the Mosses again. We need a fast ride to Juneau. Yes, from right where you left us." She paused. "Okay, that's fine. Thanks."

The Mosses—I like that. It's so . . . domestic. And what was the 'Okay, that's fine' for?" Scott asked, already knowing the answer.

"The price."

"Great. Another five hundred down the drain. How quick?"

"Quickly. They'll be here in under an hour."

"Well, that certainly will be quickly."

"Scott, I can't deal with your antics right now. I just saw a dead woman staring at me and it's made me feel very unsteady. Please stop."

"I'm sorry."

"You didn't see her up close."

"I know. I'm sorry."

"Her face was pure white and her eyes were wide open. It was horrible."

"I'm so sorry."

"Stop it!"

"I'm sorry, I don't know what else to say."

"You can stop saying you're sorry. You're making me angry."

"You can't make . . ."

"You're *causing* me to be angry! Just stop it!" Julia was off the boat the second it touched Earl's dock, and headed for Millie's at a march.

Scott turned to Earl." You'll give your bill to the Alaska State Troopers, right?"

"Yep. Two days—four hundred bucks. As per our agreement," Earl said with a wink and a smile.

"You think they'll buy that?"

"Hell yes. This is exciting stuff." Earl started organizing his gear. "They won't bat an eye."

Scott skipped after Julia, shaking his head.

They packed in silence, went to the field, and waited for the helicopter.

Chapter 7
He Knows *Of* You

Juneau Airport wasn't small, but it wasn't too big, either. It *was* awash in passengers. A few State Troopers were checking every airline.

"Oh jeez. This won't go well, or quickly," Scott said. "We need some kind of a break." He put their suitcases on a baggage carousel and started for the departures area. "Our bags can go around for a while. They'll be safe."

"What are we looking for?" Julia asked.

"The wheelchair. They won't need it now that they're on the lam. The concourse first, and then the parking lots."

"You're not so dumb, are you?"

"You start from that end, I'll start from the far end. Look behind everything then hit the parking lots, okay? We'll meet somewhere in the middle." Scott took off running.

Two hours later, they met. "Nothing?"

"I'm sorry, Scott," Julia said, "But we're way overdue for some food. How about we take a short break and get something to eat?"

"We can grab a sandwich inside."

"No, I need to sit down for at least twenty minutes. Running through the airport after two days of dives has really drained me. There's a pretty nice restaurant in the center. Why don't we eat there?"

"Fine." Scott started to run inside.

"Hey!" Julia snapped.

He stopped. "What?"

"I'm tired! What part of that wasn't clear?"

Scott swept his arm toward the terminal. "At your pace, milady."

They walked into the restaurant and stopped cold. There, collapsed against the back wall, was the wheelchair. "Of course. They couldn't leave it on the boat or on the bus. Somebody would see it. But they could leave it in a crowded restaurant full of strangers. Who would notice?" Scott scanned the tables for them. "And now they're long gone."

"We should have eaten first," Julia groaned.

Scott grabbed two napkins and wheeled the chair out into the concourse. "How much can you do on your magical iPhone?"

"Everything." Julia zipped to Google. "What do you need to know?"

"Wheelchair manufacturers."

"Okay. Over six thousand results in a third of a second. What now?"

Scott was searching the wheelchair for a name. "Find Graham Field Health Products.

"Got it—Denver."

"Okay, let's go."

"What about food?"

"Later." Scott copied the serial number and wheeled the chair out to a State Trooper. "Officer, this is the chair that the two murderers you're looking for abandoned. It may still have prints on it. I was careful not to touch it."

Julia watched a young man walk by eating a giant pretzel with mustard on it. She groaned.

"Who are you?" the officer asked.

"Name's Moss. Officer Bunch probably called."

"He did, Mr. Moss. You were supposed to stay put. He needs your statement."

"He already got it. I think the murderers are headed for Denver. That's where the wheelchair came from. That's out of your jurisdiction so you'll probably need to inform the FBI." Scott was off in a flash. "Gotta run."

"Hey! Wait a minute!" The officer was left holding the chair.

~~~~~~~~~~~

Mr. Butane and the fake Mrs. Butane never used their return tickets. They flew to Seattle instead. Under a different name.

~~~~~~~~~~~

Scott bought tickets, proved his cameras were cameras at the scanning station, and they headed down the concourse. As they ran for the plane, Julia searched her memory. "The Denver FBI. Didn't you screw up one of their agent's vacations a while

93

back? Didn't he get on a plane and get in a fight with an air marshal or something?" Julia asked.

"No, that was a guy from San Diego. I don't know any agents in Denver, so he won't know me."

"Aren't you lucky." Julia smirked.

"Yeah, I get to make a new friend in Denver."

Julia's answer was a sputter.

They were the last passengers to board the flight. "Just made it," Scott said.

"Should I look for a suspicious woman on this flight?" Julia asked with sarcasm.

"No. One per week is about all we can handle."

"Some honeymoon," Julia quipped.

"Think do-over."

"Maybe we can go somewhere where there aren't any people."

"Always a possibility."

"Right." Julia closed her eyes and fell over on Scott's shoulder.

~~~~~~~~~

The Denver FBI agent, William Stulberg, met Scott and Julia at the airport security office. "You're Mr. Scott Moss, correct?"

"You can call me Scott," Scott said pleasantly, and stuck out his hand.

Agent Stulberg ignored his hand. "You can call me Agent Stulberg," he said, coldly.

"Uh, oh," Scott mumbled.

Julia bit her tongue. "I'm Julia Moss. It's nice to meet you." She stuck out her hand.

"Hello." Stulberg shook her hand and headed for parking. "You can fill me in on the way to my car. I'm in official parking."

Julia called her office.

Scott stared at his un-shook hand for a moment and followed. "We're going to rent a car, Agent Stulberg. We'll meet you at your office, okay?"

"Suit yourself." He handed Julia a card. "You can Google a map." He smiled at Julia. "Nice to meet you, Mrs. Moss." Then turned and left.

Scott watched him stride away. "Ohhh, this is going to be very unpleasant."

Julia watched him go. "Well, somehow, some way, he knows *of* you."

"I guess. Not very encouraging."

"No new friend for you." Julia headed for the rental car counters.

~~~~~~~~~~

The Denver office of the FBI got a call from the Alaska State Troopers. The wheelchair had been wiped clean of fingerprints. Ron McDonnell, the chief steward, had disappeared completely. Butane was a bogus name. "It's nothing you wouldn't expect," Agent Stulberg said, "If there *was* a murder, it was a well-planned murder."

"Ronald McDonald? Really?" Scott asked.

"Just Ron—middle name Lon," Stulberg said, "And it's McDonnell, not McDonald."

"His name is Ron Lon McDonnell?"

"It's Alaska," Stulberg said.

"Okay, why the cold reception? Do I know you from somewhere?"

"Is that all it takes? Just knowing you?" Agent Stulberg asked.

Julia involuntarily nodded *yes*.

"Come on. What's up?" Scott asked.

Stulberg stared at Scott for a minute. "Do you remember a while back? When those clowns tried to blow up Disneyland?"

"Ohh, right." Scott pointed. "You were going to be my replacement."

"I was, but I couldn't get out of Denver. Special Agent Scraper was going crazy trying to find you." Stulberg paused. "And I knew his predecessor Somersby before he went over to Homeland Security. And one of our guys in San Diego almost lost his job because of some mix-up on a plane. I don't want to go crazy—or lose my job, that's all."

Scott shrugged. "Well, okay. As long as it isn't anything serious."

Julia could see Stulberg's spring tightening. "Things are better now, Agent Stulberg, Scott's married now. He's settling down."

"Terrific." Stulberg kept it businesslike. "Fill me in. You believe the man who may or may not have killed his wife in Alaska is somewhere here in the Denver area?"

"Oh, I'm sure he did it, Agent Stulberg. The wheelchair he pushed his wife around in came from here. So it's a good bet."

"Well, it's a reasonable bet," Julia added.

"What else?"

"I got the serial number. I thought we could find the buyer from that."

Stulberg held out his hand. "Very good. That'll be very helpful. Can you think of anything else that might help prove there was a murder?"

"Not off hand. But we can go through the files at the manufacturer. If they . . ."

"No," Stulberg interrupted. "There won't be any *we,* Moss. The FBI will take over now." Stulberg continued holding out his hand. "If you'll just give me the serial number, please."

Scott balked. "Ease up there, G-man. What did I ever do to you?"

"Nothing. And I'm hoping to keep it that way. The number, please?"

"Fine." Scott copied the number onto Stulberg's pad. "Could you at least keep us informed? I *am* the one who found the body."

"Really? The Alaska State Troopers didn't say anything about that."

"Would you? If you were them?"

Stulberg stared for a moment. Then almost nodded. "Fine. I'll keep you informed."

"Good," Julia said and handed Stulberg her card. "You can reach Scott or me at this number."

Stulberg stared at her card, still very cool and businesslike. "You'll be going back to LA, then?"

"Probably." Scott started backing away. "We'll let you know."

Stulberg suddenly tensed.

Scott and Julia were out the door before he could say anything more.

"If you were they."

"What?" Scott asked.

"You said 'them'. It's, 'If you were they'."

"Really? That sounds gay."

"It sounds correct. And what have you got against gays, all of a sudden?"

"Hey! Clair, my secretary, is gay."

"No she's not. I've met her husband."

"Okay, that was wrong. I surrender. We need to get to Graham Field before Stulberg does."

"Of course we do," Julia said, dryly.

They ran to their rental car and OnStar quickly got them to Graham Field Health Products offices.

They burst through the door, startling the young woman at the front desk.

Scott showed the serial number to the young gal. "We'd like to know who owns this wheelchair. Who do we see?"

"Whom," Julia said.

"Yes. Whom as well."

A little taken back, the young woman picked up her phone. "You'll want Mr. Axel." She waited a moment. "Mr. Axel we have a couple out here who need assistance finding the owner of a chair. "There seems to be some urgency."

"Aren't you going to correct her?" Scott asked. "Give her the old who-whom business?"

"No. In that particular context, she said it right." Julia answered back.

"Correctly," Scott corrected.

"Touché."

"Gesundheit."

The woman's eyes shot back and forth. "Is this on Candid Camera?"

"No—you're on Candid Grammar. She's the host." Scott winked.

"We're tired. We're supposed to be in Alaska. On our honeymoon," Julia said.

"But we're taking a Murphy."

"That's a do-over."

"His fault."

"You started it."

"Did not."

The gal stared at them for a moment, then looked around. "Come on, is there a camera?"

"I'm Mr. Axel. How can I help you?" Mr. Axel had walked up behind them.

Scott turned and handed him the serial number. "Can you tell us who owns this chair?"

Axel looked at the slip for one second. "Yes, I can. Mr. Butane bought it with cash, a month ago. He insisted it be this exact model."

"Holy crap!" Scott was astounded.

"Another FBI agent called and asked about this same number just twenty minutes ago. Are you both on this . . .?"

"Oh! Yeah." Scott recovered. "We sometimes get our wires crossed. I thought agent Stulberg was following another lead."

"Stulberg. Yes, that was his name."

Scott hesitated, then asked, "So, Mr. Axel, do you sell a lot of this model?"

I'd have to look that up. Do you need it right away, or can I email it to your office?"

"We'd like to wait for the information, if you wouldn't mind."

"It'll just take a minute. You want the number of units sold, correct?"

"And the names of the customers, if you can. As far back as a year. We're pretty sure Butane is a false name. The chair he bought was a second chair to disguise an illegal activity. We need to find the first chair he bought under his real name."

"Ohhh . . . that'll take a bit longer."

"We'll wait."

"You didn't say you were FBI," the gal behind the desk said.

"That's right, I didn't. I'm sorry."

"Ohh, brother." Julia sat down on the waiting room couch. When Scott joined her she said, "Impersonating an FBI officer. We'll never be able to come back to Denver, ever again."

"No. She said I hadn't told her that I was FBI, and I agreed with her—I'm not FBI."

Julia opened a magazine to hide her amusement. "The way you can twist words, you would have been a great defense lawyer."

Axel was out with the list fifteen minutes later. "Should I send a copy to your office?"

"One copy is enough, thanks. The files get too fat as it is." Scott and Julia hotfooted it out of there.

"Add obstruction of justice," Julia said. "Trump would be so proud."

"Who says we're not going to give the FBI this list when we're done? Let's hope Agent Stulberg isn't smart enough to ask for one."

"He will, you know."

"But hopefully not until after he tries to find the mythical Mr. Butane."

"That won't take more than an hour."

"So we have to hurry." He handed Julia the paper. "How many in the Denver area?"

"Hundreds."

"Just the rich areas. Butane didn't look poor. Maybe we can catch him with his pants down."

"How about Cherry Hill?"

"As good a place to start as any."

"Stulberg is going to do the same thing, you know? He's going to ask for this list, and your Mr. Axel is going to tell him he gave it to the other agent. And Stulberg is going to know he gave it to you, even though you didn't give Axel your name."

"So we have to *really* hurry."

OnStar directed Scott and Julia from house to house. Scott would run up, ring the doorbell, and when the homeowner wasn't Mr. or Mrs. Butane, Scott would leave instantly, saying, "So sorry to bother you, wrong number."

One hour and twenty "So sorrys" later, Julia's phone rang. "Hello?"

"This is Agent Stulberg, Mrs. Moss. Please put Mr. Moss on."

Julia handed Scott the phone. "Stulberg. Buckle up," she whispered.

Scott cringed and said, "Hello, Agent Stulberg." He listened. "No, I never said I was an FBI agent. He just assumed it."

"Told you," Julia said.

Scott waved her off. "No, that's not true. I'm not obstructing anything. I'm helping."

"Told you."

Scott waved again. "Well, that may be true, but isn't the murder of a woman more important than a few bends in the rules?"

"We're finished in Denver," Julia said. "And I was hoping to ski here some day."

Scott waved at her again. "I am too helping. Look, I can give you a list of the homes we've already checked that aren't the murderers." Scott cringed. "That's awfully harsh Agent Stulberg. Okay, okay, fine, check them out yourself. Sorry, I have to go." Scott hung up. "He's really pissed. He called me a horse's ass."

"They shoot horses' asses, don't they?" Julia said with a smile.

"He has to catch me first."

The very next OnStar address had a "For Sale" sign with a "Sold" banner on it. Julia stopped, abruptly. They looked at each other. "So, Sherlock, what do you think?" she asked.

"I think he's smart," Scott said. "I couldn't figure out how he was going to explain a new wife to everybody when they returned from their trip. And I'm Watson, not Sherlock."

"He's more than smart, Watson, he's brilliant."

"No kidding, Sherlock. He just changed wives in the middle of a marriage. And he doesn't have to explain it to anybody. They move to a new town, settle in as husband and wife, and no one will ever know the difference."

"How do you suppose he got his real wife to go along with all this? Selling the house, a cruise right in the middle of it? What's the catch?" Julia asked.

"Maybe she was one of those obedient types. You know, do whatever he says, types."

"Maybe they're both on the lam, and he felt like the whole *wife in a wheelchair* was slowing him down or something." Julia said.

"As good a theory as any." Scott answered.

Julia asked OnStar to get them to the real estate office. "We have to find out where he moved." She photographed the sign with her phone.

"I'll bet he's got that covered too."

"Yes, but he slipped up somewhere."

"Atta girl."

"Do you think Agent Stulberg will figure it out? If we run into him at the real estate office, he'll probably arrest you."

"He might, but he's about a hour behind us. Maybe more if he chases after the mythical Butane for a while. We should be gone by then."

"Good luck with that."

"Let's keep a positive attitude, Jules. He's on a phone—we're working the street. We're at least an hour ahead of him."

"Hold that thought."

~~~~~~~~~~

Scott and Julia zipped into the parking lot and barged through the door of the real estate office.

"Hi there!" Scott said.

"Hi! I'm Susan Shimmer, what can I sell you today? We're featuring a 'two for one' special on downtown condominiums all this week." The real estate lady waited for their reaction.

Scott and Julia stopped and stared at her.

"That usually gets a laugh," Susan said.

"Ha ha?" Scott said.

"Seriously though, what are you in the market for? Are you planning to buy or sell? Or both!"

Susan was way too perky for Julia. Julia showed Susan the photo of the sign and said, dryly, "This property just sold, correct?"

"Yes, you're too late," she said, sadly. "But I have another property just as nice," she bubbled. "Actually, *I* think it's a little nicer. It's just a few blocks from there. And it's in the same school district and everything."

"We're interested in the seller," Scott said.

"Oh. You're not in the market." Susan's bubbly demeanor slowly faded. "I'm afraid we don't give that information out. It's in the public record if you really need to know."

"Thank you." Julia turned to go.

"And if we really needed to know much faster, what could we do?" Scott asked.

"You could *race* down to public records," Susan said, sarcastically. She had already lost interest and was thumbing through her listings book.

"Oh, really?" Julia pushed up her sleeves, ready to take little Susan on.

Scott quickly took Julia's arm and turned her toward the door. "Thanks."

"I'm not finished with her yet," Julia said, resisting Scott's tug.

"Yeah, you are." Scott dragged an angry Julia toward the door.

~~~~~~~~~~~

They raced downtown, to the county offices, to public records. Scott quickly found the name. "The property belonged to Jason Fellows. How many Jason Fellows do you think there are in the United States, Jules?"

Julia was already looking it up. "Seventy-six."

"That many?"

"That's what's listed in the white pages. There could be a few more. But it won't make any difference, Scott. We may know who he is now, but he's just moved. He won't show up anywhere until he re-establishes."

"Okay, fine. But when he moves he's not going to change his name. He must have a business or a profession of some kind. He won't start over."

"You don't know that, Scott. He could have changed his name already. He used a fake name on the cruise. And he always used cash. He could be Bill Smith, living in Maine for all we know."

"Maybe. But right now, this is all we have. My money's on a similar name. Try his middle name. Jason William Fellows. JW, or William, or Bill. How many of those?"

Julia looked it up. "There are twenty-five professional people named William Fellows, one's

105

a really good actor, and endless JWs and endless Bills. There's got to be a faster way, Scott.

Scott sat for a moment. "Follow the money."

"And how do we do that?"

"Easy. We hack into something, somewhere."

"We could do that," Julia paused. "If you hadn't gone around the FBI, they would have been a big help. But now we're on our own."

"Yeah, that was a bad move on my part. Call Agent Stulberg for me would you?"

Julia punched in his number and handed her phone to him. "Here you go."

"No! I wanted you to—oh, hi, Agent Stulberg. We just found out that Jason Fellows, the murderer, just sold his house."

Agent Stulberg was standing in front of Susan Shimmer. "We don't know he's a murderer, Mr. Moss!" Stulberg barked. He took a breath to calm himself down. "That's just your speculation, isn't it? But, I am checking it out." He shot Susan a look. "As a matter of fact, I'm in Ms. Shimmer's office right now." Stulberg barked again, "And where the hell are you, dammit?"

Susan jumped every time Stulberg shouted.

"We're at public records. The killer's name is Jason Fellows. Did she tell you?"

"You don't have any proof the man is a killer. Hold on." Stulberg looked at Susan and demanded, "Is Jason Fellows the man who owned the house? I need to know NOW! This is an FBI matter!"

Frightened little Susan nodded a quick little yes. "Yes, I'm sorry."

Stulberg went back to Scott. "Meet me in my office Mr. Moss. I'll see you in half an hour."

"He's pissed." Scott handed Julia her phone. "He doesn't believe us."

"Big surprise," Julia said.

"He wants me to come in."

"Are you going to?"

"I guess I should. If I can convince him, he can trace the money a lot faster than I could."

"Not necessarily." Julia checked her watch. "It's past five on a Friday. He needs a warrant."

"So. He'll wake up a judge."

"Let's see, Scott. There was a drowning. Up in Alaska, up a river, many miles from Juneau."

"The weights prove it was murder," Scott said.

"I don't remember the divers bringing up any weights, do you?"

Scott thought about it. "Actually, no. But they could have come loose on her way down. He could have stuck them in her dress or something. They're down there—somewhere."

"Maybe. But they're probably not going to find them. And many days later a wheelchair was found in the airport restaurant, in Juneau. It actually was taken from the restaurant by you, without anyone's permission. It was one of hundreds sold this year. This one was sold to a Mr. Butane, who was seen wheeling his very alive wife off the boat in the same kind of chair, five days after the murder, after the cruise was over. Did Mr. Butane forget it? Or lose it? Or simply abandon it after his wife recovered? Is it even the same one? And what else?

107

It wasn't sold to Mr. Fellows. Plus, so far, there is no proof that Mr. Fellows was ever *in* Alaska. Do you think a judge would let the FBI go rummaging through Mr. Fellows's private life, a US citizen, on evidence that circumstantial?"

"Well, when you say it like that."

"They're going to need fingerprints off the body to even prove who the woman is."

"Was."

"Right. And if the real Mrs. Fellows is actually the victim, and has never been fingerprinted, they can't go to dental x-rays because she had false teeth, and they were missing." Julia shuddered at the vision. "And everything has to happen between the Colorado FBI and the Alaska State Troopers. By the time they get an okay from a judge, *if* they can even get one, weeks will have passed."

"Plan B," Scott quietly said.

"What's Plan B," Julia asked.

"Hope Diamond."

"The big heavy computer lady who hacked the race track files for you? Do you think she'll do it?"

"We can ask. We can't do anything here." Scott checked his watch. "I'm sure we can catch a late flight to LA. We can sleep in our own bed tonight and call Hope in the morning."

"What about Agent Stulberg? He's expecting you to come to the FBI office, you know?"

"He'll be glad we're out of his hair. Let's go."

"Terrific, he can add '*flight*' to the FBI's charges." Julia chased after him.

Chapter 8
Pie

LAX was crowded. Julia and Scott were bone tired. "I never thought I'd enjoy airline food, ever," she said, walking down the concourse. "But I actually didn't mind it."

"Hunger is the best sauce," Scott said, as they went to baggage claim.

"Who first said that?" Julia asked.

"Cervantes Saavedra," Scott answered.

Julia looked at Scott in amazement. "You're not so dumb, are you?"

Scott shrugged and smiled.

"For a flatfoot, I mean."

"Here. Drag your own bag." Scott let go of the handle and Julia rolled it out behind him, grinning.

~~~~~~~~~~~

When they got home they headed straight for the bedroom, dropped their bags and went straight to bed without turning on one light.

Scott started snoring inside three minutes.

The next morning, Scott woke up before Julia. He smiled, got up, took a trip to the bathroom, and headed for the kitchen.

Julia stirred. "No, that's okay," she said, still half-asleep, "I'll make the coffee." She struggled to get out of bed.

"You're tired, Jules. Go back to sleep. I can make the coffee."

"No, it's really okay, I love making coffee in the morning," she said as she staggered toward the kitchen. "Go take your shower."

"You just don't like the way *I* make coffee," he insisted.

"No, that's not true," she said. "I *detest* the way you make coffee. *You* can't even drink it."

After they took showers, had Julia's coffee, and ate Scott's scrambled eggs—with toast, Scott called Hope Diamond at work. He asked her if they could meet. She agreed—her break was at ten-thirty.

At ten twenty-five Scott and Julia walked up to her desk. Scott gulped. "Hope?" he questioned.

"I guess I should have said something over the phone. I lost a few pounds," Hope said, smiling.

"You look wonderful," he said.

"I'm Julia Moss." Julia stuck out her hand.

"Nice to meet you. Scott helped me a while back. So I'm glad to return the favor. I'll meet you in the break room as soon as my replacement comes." She pointed down the hall. "You can't miss it. It says employees only, but nobody cares."

"Fat, my fanny" Julia said as they went down the hall. "You spent all night with that gorgeous

110

woman and didn't have the guts to tell me." Julia surged into the break room ahead of Scott.

"Hey! She weighed at least a hundred pounds more when I spent the night with her—I mean saw her—I mean—did computer stuff—when I did the searches with her," Scott protested.

"Uh-huh."

Over coffee in the break room at the records office, Scott laid out as much as he could about the murder and the home sale. Hope looked skeptical. "That's a tall order, Scott."

"Well, we didn't have much evidence when I helped you find your husband's killer, either."

"No. Not that. I'll be happy to help you, but I don't know if I can hack into those kinds of files. It's been a long time, Scott."

"You can do it, Hope." Scott leaned back.

"Not without a dollar." Hope held out her hand.

Scott nodded and quickly found a dollar. "Boy, you look terrific."

She leaned in. "I lost almost a hundred pounds. Can you believe it?"

"Yes, I can, Hope." Scott nudged Julia. "Can you believe it, Jules?"

Julia hesitated. "Well, I don't have anything to compare to. So . . . what can I say?"

Hope pulled a snapshot out of her purse. "I keep this close to remind me." She showed her 'before' photograph to Julia.

"Wow!" Julia said and quickly added, "I mean yes, that's . . . you're . . . it's . . ."

Hope winked. "I was really fat. You can say it."

"Well, congratulations. "I'm sure you feel much better, now," Julia said.

"I really do. No more pie ala mode for me."

"Moving on," Scott said. "Where can we do this? I'd like to stay one step ahead, if we can."

"Ahead of who?" Hope asked, cautiously.

Scott hesitated. "The killer, of course."

Hope turned to Julia and tossed her head at Scott. "What's he really doing?"

"He's trying to stay ahead of the FBI," she said.

"Uh-huh." Hope shook her finger at Scott. "You haven't changed."

Scott shrugged. "They'll move too slow."

"Slowly," Julia corrected.

Hope glanced between the two. "Any computer will do," she said. "But this could take a little while so we shouldn't use a laptop. And it should be some place quiet. It's been so long I'm gonna have to really concentrate."

"How about our place, Hope? Scott and I both have computers. I'll make dinner. You could come right after work, if that's possible?"

"Okay. Thank you, Julia." Hope nodded.

"Do you need a ride?"

"No, I have my own car." She smiled, sadly. "Scooter had a very big life insurance policy. He took very good care of me."

"Scooter was a good man, Hope." Scott wrote the address on a page from his little notebook. "We'll see you right after work, then."

As they left Julia asked, "What was that dollar business all about?"

"She was dead broke. I made her pay me a dollar to help her find . . ."

"Oh! That's right," Julia interrupted. "You were trying to keep me from finding out you were back in the detective business. She lied for you."

"No, the dollar was to find Scooter's killer."

"Well, it's a dollar more than you're getting paid for this investigation," Julia said, "Why are we doing this, anyway?"

"To right a terrible wrong," Scott shrugged. "And I didn't like the hostile way he talked to me on the boat. If he'd been just a tad nicer he might have gotten away with murder."

Julia scoffed. "I'll keep that in mind if I ever decide to kill somebody."

"You're not the killer type."

"I don't know about that. I've wanted to kill you more than once."

"But you didn't. That's the difference."

~~~~~~~~~~

With Hope's, and her own figure in mind, Julia made a chef salad for dinner.

Hope had a modest portion with no dressing. "You know what's funny," she said as they ate.

"No. What's funny?" Scott asked.

"I hardly ever eat salad. This is really good."

"Thanks, Hope. It's just lettuce, carrots, eggs, ham, turkey, and a little cheese," Julia said.

"How did you lose weight, then?" Scott asked.

"Pie," Hope said. After a beat, she grinned.

113

Scott grinned along with her, but Julia was at a bit of a loss. "What's so funny about pie?"

Hope stopped and sighed. "My Scooter liked to watch me eat," she said, smiling. Then she leaned back and sighed once more. "If I could have him back, I'd eat pie again—whenever he wanted."

Awkward silence gripped all three. Julia and Hope suddenly had tears in their eyes.

"Okay! Let's have a big pot of coffee and get started," Scott said, trying to rescue the moment.

Scott and Julia sat on the couch, while Hope worked. Around midnight Julia asked, "Would you like a glass of wine, Hope? I'm going to open a bottle of merlot."

"Half a glass, thanks." Hope never looked up from Scott's computer.

"Good idea." Scott got out three wine glasses.

Hope worked on.

Around two-thirty in the morning, Hope said, "I'm sorry this is taking so long. It isn't easy."

Scott's eyes popped open. He was slumped on the couch, fast asleep. "No, that's okay, Hope. Whatever it takes." Scott rubbed his face. "Is there anything I can do to help?"

"Maybe some coffee?"

"Sure, I'll make us a pot." Scott started to get up, and Julia came stumbling out of the bedroom, a small blanket slipping off her shoulders and landing on the floor. "No!" She said desperately. "I'll make us a pot." She had curled up on the bed for a nap.

Scott shook his head. "Ohh, come on, Jules, my coffee's not that bad."

Hope looked at Julia.

Julia frowned and shook her head no.

Hope worked through the night, and Julia made breakfast in the morning. "I'm going to call in sick today," Hope said. "I'm finally getting somewhere on our illusive Mr. Fellows. " She quickly ate and got right back to hacking.

"At ten o'clock Hope leaned back. "Well, there he is—everything. His accounts, his savings, his business, his phone records, everything."

Scott quickly jumped in. "He's rich. No surprise there. He's transferred almost everything down to numbered accounts in Mexico. He's left a chunk of money in the accounts here in the States—how odd. None of the stuff in Mexico is in a name."

"He didn't put it overseas?" Julia leaned in.

Hope pushed back. "I need some sleep." She curled up on the couch and instantly fell asleep.

"Why Mexico?" Julia wondered.

"He has over eight million dollars in assets. Maybe their banks have better interest rates." Scott studied the screen. "It would appear he retired from his law practice less than six months ago. I guess he must have wanted a different wife to spend his golden years with. Or maybe he just hated his real wife." Scott shrugged.

"With which to spend his golden years." Julia corrected.

"That too," Scott said. "But why Mexico?"

"Everything is in numbered accounts, Scott. His name isn't anywhere in Mexico. Once he closes the accounts he's drained, it'll be almost impossible to trace him. He could easily transfer what is left to Canada or anywhere."

"To throw the FBI off."

"They'll probably start looking overseas instead of in Mexico. It could take them months."

"And that'll give him plenty of time to move the numbered accounts around down there. A couple of transfers and they're gone. He's brilliant."

"Uh-oh," Julia said, darkly.

"Uh-oh, what?" Scott asked, slightly alarmed.

"What if where he's going, he's going alone."

It took a beat for Scott to catch up to Julia's thought. "The new wife's expendable. He needed a fake wife to make the transition. He'll pay her off or kill her before he resurfaces." Scott checked his phone records. "There are four calls to a moving company. His furniture is going somewhere."

Julia was on the phone in an instant. "Allied Movers, I need to check on our furniture. Can you tell us where it is right now? The name's Fellows. Yes, Jason and Joyce Fellows." Julia pushed Scott away from the screen. "The number? Let me see, I have it here somewhere." She studied the screen. "I can't seem to find it. And I can't seem to find the check number we paid you with. I guess I'm not much help?" Julia suddenly snapped her fingers. "You know, what? Try Mr. Jerald Butane. Jason sometimes uses his stage name—he thinks it gives him more publicity—*I* think it's stupid. Yes, he does very elaborate magic shows. He makes things disappear—people, wheel chairs, you name it. But can't you . . . thank you."

116

"Very clever girl," Scott said. "But it's 'with which we paid'."

Julia covered the phone and stuck her tongue out at Scott. "They're looking for it."

"Get a delivery date," Scott said.

"A cashier's check, no wonder I couldn't find it. Sunshine Storage. And when is it . . . already? Thank you. My husband just forgot to tell me." She hung up. "They unloaded it a week ago. Sunshine Storage, in Florida."

"And yet everything he has financially, is in Mexico. How strange," Scott said.

"Unless . . ." Julia paused.

"He has no intention of ever picking the stuff up." Scott finished her thought.

"Eight million buys a lot of new furniture," Julia said. "He's leaving the authorities a dead end."

"Wouldn't they check the moving company?"

"Sure. But there, he used the name Mr. Butane. They'll wait for Butane to come for his furniture. By then Fellows will be in Mexico."

"And Mexico's a big country," Scott said.

"The FBI is going to find all this out. Probably the same way Hope did, you know?"

"Yes, eventually. And they're going to stake out Sunshine Storage forever. But, with numbered accounts, I'll bet the banks in Mexico aren't going to be all that cooperative. They'll assume the FBI is tracing drug money and be fairly unwilling to get sideways with the cartels. Most of the bank

117

officials probably have children and they'll drag their collective feet—maybe forever."

"That's awful, Scott." Julia shuddered. "But the FBI will certainly tell the banks in Mexico they're looking for a killer, not drugs."

"Maybe. But we're getting ahead of ourselves." Scott paused. "If the body is never identified as the real Mrs. Fellows, the FBI will have no excuse to pursue Mr. Fellows. And Mr. Butane was seen with his wife long after the murder. If they check, people on the boat undoubtedly saw them together after the first night. And for the whole rest of the trip."

"And besides that," Julia added, "There's no proof the body was ever on that boat—or any boat, for that matter. She'll be a Jane Doe issue at best. And if no one is looking, or asking about Ms. Doe, who's going to care? Right now Agent Stulberg is chasing Fellows on your say-so."

"Which won't last," Scott said. "I don't think he was ever convinced it really was a murder. In any case, he'll have no legal authority to chase Fellows if the body can't be identified. If anybody, he'll end up looking for Jerald Butane."

"Not really. If the body can't be identified, or if the weights are never found, it's an unknown person, drowned in an Alaskan river. It's not an FBI case. No looking for Butane, no looking for Fellows, no nothing." Julia paused. "Ohh, he's good," she said.

"He's really good."

~~~~~~~~~~

Scott and Julia had no way of knowing Jason Fellows had never returned to Denver.

Jason met with Ron Lon McDonnell at the Original Starbucks in Seattle. "No one knows you came down here, right?"

"No. I slipped off the boat and shot down here without telling anyone. But I have a big problem. This was supposed to be quick and easy. That Scott Moss makes everything more complicated. If he starts looking, I'm not going to have anywhere safe that I can go. I'm going to need a lot more money than you're paying me."

"How much more? Fellows sounded cold.

Ron hesitated. "I know you're rich."

"Yeah, so?"

Ron swallowed hard. "I'm going to need at least Five hundred thousand."

Jason Fellows stared at his collaborator with no expression whatsoever. After a minute, he softened his attitude, nodded, and said, "Okay, Ron. I guess, under the circumstances, that's not unreasonable."

"I'll have to change my name and occupation. And I'll need a new place to live, so . . ."

"I get it," Jason said. "But I only brought the ten thousand we agreed on. And when I pay you the five hundred thousand, you have to put it in the bank, or market, or wherever, a little at a time. That much money will cause suspicion anywhere, unless you put it overseas. That's actually best." Fellows smiled. "If you want, I could help you do that. I have some very private connections overseas."

"Okay." Ron breathed a little easier. "I thought you might not understand my problem. Thanks for being so reasonable."

"Hey! Ron! I *do* understand," Jason said, being very agreeable. "And I sure don't want anything to happen to you that would lead back to me." He paused for a moment. "But, it's going to take me a little time to figure out how to get that much money to you." Jason looked around the coffee shop. "You know what? Let's not try to figure it out in here. There are too many ears to eavesdrop on us," he said. And as he got up he asked, "By the way, how did you get here?"

"I rented a car," Ron said.

"Good. You can drive us—I took a cab. We'll find a place where we can figure out how, when, and where, to make the transfer."

Ron got up with a light heart.

Jason Fellows left with a dark heart. He wasn't planning to surrender even ten thousand.

"Where should we go?" Ron asked.

"Someplace quiet. Where we can figure out the transfer without any disturbance. I know. How about the parking lot of a supermarket? They're innocent enough, nobody pays any attention, and they're pretty much everywhere."

Ron smiled as he drove off. "I'm on it."

~~~~~~~~~~

Around noon Julia asked, "What are we going to do, Scott? Tell Agent Stulberg all this, and try to get the help of the FBI, or what?"

Scott was still pondering the information on the computer screen. "Stulberg has no reason to believe us. He'll be fairly agitated. Especially after I went around him and got Butane's real name before he did. And he just might throw us in jail for hacking into Fellows's accounts."

Still asleep on the couch, Hope's eyes popped open. "Who's going to jail? I'm not going to jail!"

"No, no, no! You were never here, Hope. This is between Agent Stulberg and Jules and me."

"Hey!" Julia shouted.

Scott patted the air. "Everybody just relax. He'll probably let the whole thing drop. And leave the investigation to the Alaska State Troopers."

"So, where does that leave us?" Julia asked.

"Free to catch a murdering bastard, I guess." As he was saying it, the phone rang. Scott looked at the caller and said, "Uh-oh, it's our favorite FBI agent, Nick Scraper. This could get complicated." He took a deep breath, picked up, and started talking really fast. "Before you say anything—I had no choice. There isn't anything except circumstantial proof. So, because the FBI couldn't legally pursue it, I was forced to look into it. It was my civic duty." Then he waited for Nick's expected tirade.

None came.

Scott listened. "Hello? Nick? Are you there?"

Special Agent Nick Scraper of the FBI was very calm. "There's no such thing as circumstantial *proof*, Scott. It's proof, or it isn't. And what the hell did you do to Agent Stulberg? He was so furious I couldn't make any sense out of what he was screaming about. Alaska? Denver? Drowning? Wheelchairs? Then some fellows sold somebody named Butane a house? What the hell's going on? He doesn't know you like I do. He wanted me to find you and shoot you on the spot. And aren't you supposed to be on your honeymoon? What are you doing back here?"

"We were on our honeymoon, but something came up, Nick. We had to come back."

"Ohh, this'll be good." Nick picked up a pencil.

"Okay, we boarded a riverboat cruise in Alaska for our honeymoon. A couple came on—she was in a wheelchair. We both heard a splash at three in the morning the first night out. The next morning she was somebody else. She was almost the same, but slightly different—perkier. Jules noticed it too."

Nick was scribbling notes on a pad. "Is Julia there? Put her on, please."

Scott handed her the phone. "He says he wants to talk to you."

Julia shook her head as she took the phone. "Hello, Nick. How are you?" Julia listened for a moment. "Yes, so far he's correct." She handed the phone back to Scott. "He says, go on."

Scott went on, "I semi-confronted him, and he got very angry."

Nick was still calm. "There's no such thing as *semi-confront*, Scott. You did or you didn't."

"Unimportant detail. The captain ordered us to leave him alone, so we left the boat, went back to where the boat was at three in the morning, and found her, drowned. Jules and Earl dove for two days and found her at the bottom of the river."

"Put Julia back on, please."

"Hi, Nick."

"You dove for two days? In icy water?"

"Earl gave me cold-water scuba gear."

"Ohh. Who's Earl? Never mind, give me Scott."

Scott took the phone. "Okay, so we traced the man back to Denver, where he just sold his house and moved. He moved all his money—eight million—down to Mexico, and he shipped his furniture to Florida to throw everybody off his trail. So far we haven't found out where he and his fake wife are. Jules worries that he may kill or abandon her if we don't catch up to him soon. He may have dumped her already. He just needed a fake wife to take the real wife's place on the boat. He would be seen with her for a week, have an alibi, leave the boat, and then she was expendable."

"Julia, please," Nick said.

She took the phone. "Nick?"

"Is he reasonably close to the truth, Jules?"

"Spot on, actually."

Nick Scraper sat, tapping his pencil on his desk. Finally he said, "Okay, I'll finish up with Scott."

Julia handed him the phone. "Go."

"And the woman had false teeth, which were washed away by the swift currents in the river, or more likely taken away by her killer on purpose. So, if she has no dental signature, if she was never fingerprinted, she's a Jane Doe. Anyway, with no actual proof of wrongdoing, the FBI can't go after this Fellows. He's just a guy who sold his house."

"Who's the guy? What house? And how many fellows are there?"

"There's only one. The man who killed his wife and moved to somewhere in Mexico, we think. That's his name—Fellows.

On his pad, Nick scribbled a capital F over the small f in fellows. Then crossed out the words *How many?* "Okay, let's see what we have here." He studied his notes. "An unidentified woman was found, drowned, in a river in Alaska, and a man named Mr. Fellows sold his house in Denver. Plus there was a couple on the weeklong river cruise named Butane. She was in a wheelchair. And you heard a splash. Those are the facts, correct?"

"Well, when you say it like that, Nick."

"How else is there to say it, Scott?"

"Well, for one thing, the woman in the chair looked much perkier in the morning. That's a fact."

"That's an opinion, Scott, not a fact. A good night's sleep can perk anybody up."

Scott hesitated. "I know it's thin."

"Thin? It's microscopic." Nick tapped his pencil a while longer. "I'm not going to ask you how you got his financial information, Scott. I don't want to have to throw you in jail."

124

"Thanks, Nick."

"Don't mention it. And I do mean don't mention it—to anybody—got it?"

"Yeah, I got it."

"Good. I have to get back to Stulberg. I'll calm him down somehow, and I'll talk to you later." Nick slammed the phone down.

"He's on our side," Scott said.

"And yet, he knows you so well." Julia scoffed.

"Hey, I helped him crack quite a few big cases. Those illegal organ transplants, tied to Scooter Diamond's death. The guns for drugs case where they threw that guy off the roof."

"Ohh, I remember. You destroyed my car."

"Yeah, that was kinda bad."

"Kinda bad? My car was bent in half and burned to a cinder! There was nothing left and I . . ."

"Whoa," Scott interrupted. "We got you a brand new car, didn't we?"

"It took weeks. Who was the dead guy—the guy who went off the roof? Did you ever find out?"

"I honestly can't remember. Plus I helped them put away Tony Bendouski for killing his wife?"

"I get it. You two have history."

"Yeah, we do. Putting away Tony Bendouski made Somersby famous."

"Well, don't break your arm patting yourself on the back, Scott."

"Hey, I helped out a lot. And that international money laundering case helped make Nick Scraper head of the department."

"Right, Zerovsky. Him, I remember. He was that crazy Russian janitor who tried to blackmail some international company, and got stabbed in the neck—sitting in the back row of that dreadful movie you took me to."

"No, you picked the movie. And the victim was Zerovsky's twin brother, the con artist. Not Zerovsky, the janitor. He went insane and shot and killed one of your kidnappers right in front of the cops." Scott smiled and nodded agreement.

"And then you got shot in Panama, by one of the other kidnappers."

"Actually, I got shot in the side. Wanna see?" Scott started to lift his shirt.

Julia grabbed his hand up to stop him. "No, thank you. I've seen it."

~~~~~~~~~~

Back in Seattle, Ron Lon McDonnell's body would spend the night in a storm sewer behind a supermarket in the suburbs.

Jason drove Ron's rental car to the Space Needle, where he picked up his fake wife, Beverly.

Ron, stripped of all identification, would move slowly along the storm sewer with each new rain. He would eventually wash out to sea, some time after the third or fourth rainstorm.

Beverly would spend many, many days and many, many months in the trunk of Ron's rental car—parked inside an All American Storage unit—paid for in cash—a full year in advance.

126

Many months after the storage rent would have run out, her remains would be discovered—quite spectacularly—on a cable TV show, live, in front of millions. The contents of that particular storage unit would be bid on—won in very spirited bidding—and the unit would then be opened. After almost two years in the metal building, in the very hot automobile trunk, Beverly's decomposing body would be unidentifiable. And the TV show would see a ten-fold jump in the ratings. The car would be traced back to Ron Lon McDonnell. But nothing would be discovered to tie the incident to the drowning of a Jane Doe in Alaska.

Mr. McDonnell would be wanted for car theft, and suspicion of murder. And his file would remain an open and very cold case.

~~~~~~~~~~

But now—before any of that could unfold— Nick called Agent Stulberg in Denver to calm him down. An hour-long conversation later, Nick called Scott, and ordered Scott to meet him downtown.

Chapter 9
A Frog in a Blender

Nick arranged to meet Scott at a nearby deli. "Sit down, Mr. Moss," he said dryly when Scott showed up.

"Still don't want to be seen with me, I guess." Scott dropped into the booth.

Nick held up two fingers when the waitress came over. "Two coffees." He turned to Scott. "I need to keep this unofficial," Nick said. "I got the full story out of Stulberg after he calmed down. And there's not enough evidence for the FBI to make a case, so we can't really move on it."

"But you can envision the possibilities, right?"

"Are you kidding?" Nick scoffed. "I could just as easily *envision* the possibilities in a way that suggests *you* did it."

"So, you believe there was a murder?"

"Yes—Maybe—I don't know." Nick threw up his hands. "There's so little to go on I can't help you, Scott. But I won't get in your way for the moment. And that could change."

The waitress brought their coffees.

Nick waited until she left. "Look, if anything breaks on the Jane Doe in Alaska, it would change everything. But for now, you can't break any laws, okay? For instance, hacking into that guy's records would be a federal offense. So don't do it, okay?"

"But you already know . . ."

"Tut, tut, tut," Nick interrupted. "I don't know anything. And for now, let's keep it that way. You go do whatever it is you do, and I'll check with Alaska every couple of days to see if anything changes. And you and I will meet for coffee every couple of days. You know, to catch up on things. Unofficially. Okay?"

"Okay, you got it, Nick. And thanks for giving me a little room. I appreciate it."

Nick gave Scott a hard stare. "This is going to come back and bite me in the ass. I just know it." He took a quick sip of his coffee, growled quietly, and got up to leave.

Scott pointed to the coffees. "That's okay, I'll get this," he said. "Nice talking to you, Scraper," he called out. But Nick had already marched through the door and disappeared.

Scott went to his office. "Hey, Clair. How's everything? Anything urgent for me?"

"It's like Grand Central Station in here," Clair said, sarcastically. She was reading. "The school called. They found their bus parked behind an apartment building one of their poorer students lived in. He took it and was trying to sell it. He wanted to kill two birds with one theft. He doesn't like school and they don't have anything to eat. He

130

was going to buy food for his family. It seemed like a perfect solution to his problems."

"Ouch. What's going to happen to the kid?"

"The school never reported it."

"They took care of it by themselves. Good."

"They got the bus back in time for school. And they're trying to arrange for some groceries, or food stamps, or some kind of fund for the mother. And the kid gets detention."

"Well, it beats prison," Scott said. "Why don't we send a hundred dollars to the fund, okay?"

"You already did, boss." Clair kept reading her paperback. "And you sent *two* hundred dollars."

"Ohh, really? How generous of me."

"Yeah. You're a great guy."

"Right."

"So, who are you chasing right now?"

Scott showed her the photo. "This guy. He murdered his wife and threw her overboard, right in the middle of our honeymoon."

"How inconsiderate," she said, dryly.

Scott got on the telephone. "Hey, Jules, do you have any connections in Mexico?"

Julia frowned, and then said, "Well, I had dinner with Enrique Peña Nieto just last week. We're very tight. Does that help?"

"I'm serious, Jules. We've got to figure out how to operate in Mexico if we're going to catch this guy."

"How to operate in Mexico?" Julia asked. "Mexican prisons are notoriously horrible, Scott. They're not going to let you run around down there, disrupting banks and creating chaos. They'll toss you in the clink so fast *The Flash* will seem like he's moving in slow motion."

"Come on, Jules, isn't there someone you know down there that can help us?"

"*Who* can help us." Julia corrected. She thought for a moment. "Well, there is a law firm down there that we've done some business with. But I don't know any of their lawyers by name. It was mostly emails, faxes, and phone calls."

"It's a start. Pack your bag, Jules. We're going to Mexico." Scott hung up.

"No, wait!" Julia closed her eyes and dropped her head. "Not only am I never going to make partner, I'm going to get fired." Julia called her boss, head of the Langford and Lawton law firm. "Dewey, it's Julia. I'm going to need a few extra days off. Our honeymoon turned into a manhunt. No, it's just Scott. He's doing what he always does. We were on a river cruise and someone got thrown overboard and drowned."

"If I hadn't been through this before I wouldn't believe it." Dewey Langford smiled. He was reading from a huge stack of briefs on his desk. "As long as your cases are in good hands, I'm fine with you taking a few extra days, Julia. Your beau is certainly an interesting diversion." He paused, put down the brief in his hand, and asked, "Is there anything we can do to help?"

Julia took a deep breath. "Actually, there is. The murderer has skipped to Mexico. I was hoping you would let me contact our friends at . . ."

"Baca and Torres. Of course, Julia. I'll make a call. I'm sure they can set you up with some kind of office to work out of."

"In which to work," Julia whispered to herself. "Thank you, Dewey," she said. "I'll try to make sure Scott and his detective business doesn't upset anyone down there."

Dewey nodded. "Well, from your stories, I'm guessing Scott and his detecting most certainly will. But, if our friends in Mexico are as bogged down in as much paperwork as we are up here, they'll probably enjoy a little chaos."

Julia smiled warmly. "You're a peach, Dewey. Thanks for not being too upset with me."

"Not a problem, Jules. Come back safe. I can't wait to hear how it all works out." Dewey called Mario Baca, gave a very sketchy explanation of the situation, asked for the favor and got a positive response. Then he sighed and went back to his stack of briefs. He went over the paper on the top of the stack and called out, "Can somebody tell me why we're involved in this animal hospital dispute? A *dog* is suing the hospital?"

~~~~~~~~~~

The offices of Baca and Torres were very, very upscale. Mario Baca showed Julia and Scott around, and gave them an office and an English-speaking clerk, a young man named Hector Israel, to assist them in whatever it was they were working on. "Dewey said something about a murder?"

"Oh! Mr. Langford didn't tell you," Julia said. "We're after a man who may have killed his wife and moved all his money to Mexican banks."

Mario Baca didn't respond at all to the idea of them looking into a killing. "Not overseas banks? How very odd." He shrugged and left.

Hector looked to be about fifteen. His eyes lit up when Julia said, *killed his wife*. "Killed his wife? Oh, boy!" he snapped his fingers.

"Uh-oh," Scott said.

"So, what do we do first, Mrs. Moss?" Hector asked. "Do we shadow this man?"

Scott cringed.

"*We* don't do anything, Hector," Julia said. "This will mostly be a paper search." Julia held up the sheet with the numbered accounts on it. "And when Scott and I figure out where these numbered bank accounts are, we'll stake them out and try to catch the man who committed the crime."

Hector grabbed the paper and quickly scanned down it. "Holy crow, Mrs. Moss! In our country it is illegal to have this kind of information. Your laws in the US must be very different."

"It's holy cow, not crow." Julia ripped the paper from his hand, gave Scott a quick look, and said, "It's kind of hard to explain, Hector. What we're doing is . . . kind of . . . well . . . it's rather . . . how do I explain this? This isn't exactly . . ."

"Ah ha!" Hector exclaimed. "I understand, Mrs. Moss." He lowered his voice. "Num's the word."

"It's mum not num, Hector. How old are you?" Scott asked. "And what's up with your last name?"

"Twenty-three—my dad was Jewish," he said, and grabbed the paper again. "We can identify each location and . . ."

Julia grabbed it back. "You can't be involved in this, Hector. You said it yourself—this is very illegal in your country."

"But, Mrs. Moss . . ."

"Call me Julia—Jules. Everybody does."

"But Julia Jules, I can really help . . ."

"Hector!" Scott grabbed his shoulder. "Calm down—take a deep breath, and relax. You have a nice job. You don't want to screw it up." Scott paused. "What was your mother? And we all call Mrs. Moss—Jules."

"Fine—Jules." Hector took a pause. "And my mom is Catholic, so I had an interesting childhood. But you should know, Mr. Moss, that I was . . ."

"Scott. Call me Scott."

"Everybody does," Julia said with a smile.

"Fine—Scott," Hector said. "You should know that I was in a gang until I was sixteen. I got out of that life and put myself through college by running little errands for . . . shall we say . . . less than sterling citizens—many of them were in politics. I can help you."

Scott studied Hector for a moment. He glanced at Julia. She shrugged.

"Okay then," Scott said. "If we get in trouble— you know a guy."

"What guy?" Hector asked.

"No. It's just an expression we use in the States. It means you're connected."

"Ahhh, yes. More American slang." Hector nodded. "I know the guy."

"A guy." Julia said with some amusement.

Hector snapped his fingers. "A guy."

Julia sat at the desk and studied the paper. Hector looked at it from upside down. "Those are numbers from the same bank," he said. "All three numbers are from the Bank of Mexico."

Julia stared at him. "How . . ."

"They use certain sequences. I recognized the bank from the first three numbers."

Julia looked. "But the numbers aren't the same."

"Not in the same order, but they identify the bank just the same. In any order, those three numbers are for the Bank of Mexico. But they won't let you withdraw from the account. There's also a hidden number that only the owner knows. That's what lets you do that. With that number you can only put money in—not take it out."

"How do you know all this?" Scott asked.

"Like I said, I ran errands for people. Politics and banking are blood brothers down here."

"You left one group out," Scott quipped.

"It's best not to mention *them,*" Hector said.

Scott thought for a minute. "Okay, we can't take money out. So . . ."

"So . . . we do what?" Julia asked.

"We make him crazy," Scott answered.

Hector snapped his fingers. "I like it."

"How do we do that?" Julia asked.

"Yes, how?" Hector asked.

136

"We put money in," Scott smiled.

"Whose money!" Julia asked with alarm.

"Yes, whose?" Hector asked.

"Not ours. Hope can help us use the money he left in his accounts back in the States."

"How do we hope for that?" Hector asked.

"Hope's a girl—a computer expert. She's a good friend who knows her way around the Internet's back channels," Scott said.

Hector snapped his fingers. "I like this Hope."

Scott nodded. "So do I, Hector. With Hope's help we can probably do a simple transfer. We'll put in amounts that let him know he's not safe."

"Like?" Julia waited.

Hector snapped again. "Yes. Like what?"

Scott snapped his fingers the way Hector did and pointed at him. "Like a deposit in the amount of the street address of the house he just sold."

"That's diabolical," Julia said.

"Yes, diabolical," Hector snapped. "Why is it, diabolical?" he asked eagerly.

"It's something that will jump out at him," Scott said. "And another deposit in an amount the same as his old phone number. And his . . . what?"

"Where did he work? We can use his badge number," Hector said.

And as Hector started to snap his fingers, Scott grabbed his hand. "No badge, but yes, we can use his law office address, or his work number. We have them all." Scott got on the phone. "May I speak to Hope Diamond, please."

"Will she be able to do that?" Julia asked.

"We'll know in a minute."

"One minute? This Hope must be the fastest computer expert in America." Hector said.

Scott smiled. "American slang again, Hector. It means pretty quick."

"Quickly." Julia corrected.

~~~~~~~~~~

Hope was on the phone, nodding, writing down numbers. "Okay, I got them. Yeah, I'm pretty sure I can do it. But why such odd amounts, Scott?" She screwed up her face. "His old address? Okay." She listened some more. "Monday, then Wednesday, then Friday, got it. The second week, the second number, okay. And the third number the third week, got it." She smiled. "No, I don't want to know why. Hey, do I care why Uncle Ben makes white rice?" Hope hung up. "He's crazier than a frog in a blender." Hope made a startled face and held her hands out like she was pressing the sides of the glass to keep from falling into the blades.

~~~~~~~~~~

"She said she'd do it." Scott hung up. "Now all we have to do is wait for our Mr. Fellows to come by the bank to find out what's happening."

"Stake out." Hector snapped his fingers. Then quickly put his hand behind his back. "Oops."

"I can't stay away that long, Scott. I have to get back to my cases."

138

"Can you stay a couple of days, at least?"

"Nothing's going to happen in two days, Scott. He probably won't even notice the deposits for a week. Maybe longer."

"So we can make this kind of a honeymoon." The minute he said it he was sorry. "I mean . . ."

"What *do* you mean, Scott?" Julia wasn't mad. She had used her serious cross-examination voice.

"I mean that was the dumbest thing I ever said."

"Not even close. But it's in the top ten."

"Is anybody hungry?" Hector suddenly asked.

"Saved by the bell," Julia said, dryly.

"Ahh. More American slang," he said. "What does it mean?"

"It means we're going to eat," Scott answered. "How about a nice family restaurant? Something local, nothing touristy."

"Hold on, Scott." Julia raised a finger.

Hector nodded in agreement. "Mrs. Jules is right. You want tourist food. The local food is not good for you. It's cheap and it's plain and it's all one color." He snapped his fingers. "Not for you." He froze, then looked at his hand. "I can't stop."

"Okay, Hector," Scott agreed. "You win."

"I'm Jules, Hector. Not Mrs. Jules." Julia picked up her purse. "Lead on."

Chapter 10
That Place Where We Had That Thing

Jason Fellows, now Jackson Bellows, stood on his deck overlooking the ocean. He sighed, picked up the *San Diego Union Tribune* and scanned the sports page. "I had to give up the Broncos for the Chargers?" He slowly shook his head, "how utterly sad for me," then tossed the paper on a deck chair and stepped inside his newly leased beach house. He stood for a while, looking around at the emptiness. "Shit!" he finally yelled. Then he made a phone call, and twenty minutes later a cab pulled up in front. "Take me to the nearest Cadillac dealer, please." It took him about twenty minutes to lease a brand new Cadillac and drive it to the nearest bar.

~~~~~~~~~~~~~

Scott took Julia to the airport and saw her off. Hector followed in his Chevy. Scott turned in his rental and hopped into Hector's car. "Thanks for doing this. I'd keep the car, but it's on my dime."

"American slang?"

"That's right," Scott said. "It means I'm paying for this effort myself."

"You're chasing this man for free? In Mexico very little is done for free," Hector said.

"It's hard to explain. The guy pissed me off."

"Ah! Vendetta. This I understand."

"I guess that's pretty close, Hec." Scott thought for a moment. "Is it okay to call you Hec?"

"In my old gang, they called me Izzy."

"Okay, Hec. Izzy works for me."

Hector drove for a while and then said, "I was the only Jewish Mexican in the whole gang."

Scott tried to hide his smile. A minute later Scott said, "Quite a distinction, Izzy."

Hector shrugged. After another mile he asked, "What do we do next?"

"I guess we wait. Where would this killer go to check on his accounts?"

"The main branch, I guess."

"We'll go there and hope we see him going in or coming out. I'll show you his picture—we can take shifts watching."

"A stakeout." Izzy raised his fingers to snap.

Scott grabbed them. "You got it."

~~~~~~~~~~

Scott would take the first four business hours and Izzy would take the next four. After a week they switched to two-hour shifts. Two weeks of waiting and watching brought no success.

Izzy looked drained and bored when Scott came to relieve him in the middle of the third week. "This isn't working."

"You're right, Izzy. Let's go back to my hotel and call Hope. Maybe she can patch us in so we can check his accounts again. Maybe we can figure something else out."

"Mum's the word still, right?"

"Ohh, yeah."

Hope didn't see any activity at all. Except for her periodic deposits, the accounts sat, quietly collecting large amounts of interest.

~~~~~~~~~~

While Scott and Izzy had been spending their days in Mexico City, sitting in front of the Bank of Mexico, Jackson had been spending his days in San Diego, staring out at the Pacific Ocean. Each night he'd watch the sunset and spend the rest of his evening in a nearby bar.

Scott called Julia every night and spent an hour on the phone. They would catch up on everything, including the sports scores. Mexican papers didn't carry much on American teams.

Julia kept Nick Scraper in the loop. He was only mildly irritated that Scott was in Mexico. "If they throw him in jail, there's not much I can do to get him out, Jules. The next time you talk to him tell him that, okay?"

"I will, Nick. But he's got a young kid helping him—an ex-gang member. I think he'll be okay."

"A gang member!" Nick's head dropped. "Of course a gang member. Who else would he hook up with?" He hung up the phone. "I knew this would come back and bite me in the ass."

Hope spent her days working, and her evenings dutifully putting the correct amounts of money into Jason's numbered accounts.

Jackson was quite buzzed the evening he finally decided to check his fortune. He was inebriated enough to not really understand the numbers he was looking at and stumbled into bed, confused. When he awoke the next morning, he was sure he'd had a bad dream. He double-checked the accounts—fixed on the three familiar deposit numbers—and slowly turned white.

~~~~~~~~~~

"Come home, Scott. It isn't working."

"Maybe I should give it a little more time," Scott said. But his heart wasn't really in it.

"Scott, do you realize we've spent exactly one night together in our apartment since we've been married? I might as well be living alone."

"I know. I'm sorry, Jules. I just don't want this guy to get away with it."

"And he won't. You'll just have to find a better way to find him, that's all."

"And how do I do that? We have to move quick or I'm afraid he'll get away."

"Quickly," Julia said. "Well, how did you find that runaway fourteen-year-old girl so fast?"

"That was easy, her walls were plastered with pictures of large animals—I found her at the zoo."

"So, what *tell* did Fellows have?"

"Nothing jumped out at me on the boat. And he cleaned out his house. I guess I could go down to Florida and check out his stuff in storage."

"You could, if you want to be arrested by the FBI in Florida. They might be sitting on it."

"Right." Scott thought. "Okay, so what do most men have in common?" Scott thought some more. "Well, I was annoyed I couldn't get any news on the Raiders down there, or any sports teams in the US. I wonder about the Denver teams. Is Fellows a sports fan? Could you have Hope check his bank statements for season tickets." Scott sighed. "I'm going to pack and get out of here. And while I'm on my way home, have her check his statements to see if he still gets a newspaper."

"You're a Raiders fan?"

"Ever since John Madden coached them. If I can't get out tonight, I'll be back tomorrow."

"Whoa, whoa. Back up. What else didn't you tell me before we got married? A *Raiders* fan? Whom do *you* have locked up in your basement?"

"Whom? Touché." Scott hung up, bid farewell to Izzy, and headed for the airport.

~~~~~~~~~~

Jackson Bellows finally had something to do during the day. He would pace, check his accounts, pace some more, and check again. He happened to be staring at the screen when Hope inserted another deposit matching his phone number. He jumped, "Ahhh!" stared in disbelief, and backed away still staring at the screen. He stumbled backward to his liquor cabinet, fumbled around, grabbed a glass and poured himself a large whisky.

~~~~~~~~~~

A short phone call and a long flight later, Julia picked Scott up at LAX.

"Hello, wife."

"Hey, Scott."

"No, hello husband?"

"Nothing's changed, Scott. We're still us."

"Okay," Scott replied. "Anything new? What's happening on our Mr. Fellows?"

"Hope is working on Jason's subscription to the *Denver Post.* They have a very good firewall."

Scott stared out the side window on the way home. "I wonder why Fellows never showed up at the bank? You'd think he would have noticed the deposits after three weeks."

"Maybe he did, but . . ." Julia paused.

"But he knew it was a setup." Scott continued to stare out the window.

"Or maybe . . ." Julia paused again.

"He just couldn't get there, or something."

"Oh my God," Julia said, quietly alarmed.

Scott stared at Julia for almost a minute. Then he felt a chill. "Ohh, jeez, you're right, Jules. He's not down there. He never was there!" Scott gently thumped the side window. "And I wasted two and a half weeks sitting on my butt in front of his bank. What a dope I was."

"If he's not down there, where is he?"

"He's got two and a half weeks on us. He could be anywhere by now. He could be in Europe, the Middle East, Hawaii, anywhere."

"Ohh. He's good."

"He's fricken diabolical. Step on it. As soon as we get home we have to email Hope and see where she is on hacking the *Denver Post*."

~~~~~~~~~~~

After three evening's efforts, Hope was finally able to find Jason on their subscription list. She emailed Scott that Jason Fellows was still getting the *Denver Post*. Then she sat, staring at the screen, waiting for a response.

Scott emailed, "Outstanding. Can you find the forwarding address?"

Hope emailed back, "No, I can't get into *Denver Post*'s addresses. That's impossible."

Scott sat for a while, thinking. He suddenly smiled and emailed, "Cancel the subscription."

"Okay." Hope said aloud. And, with a couple of dozen keystrokes, she was able to do that. *You're a devious man, Mr. Moss*, she said to herself, and emailed, "Done."

"What do we do now?" Julia asked.

"I guess we wait to see if he re-subscribes."

"And if he doesn't?"

"Well, it's a fifty-fifty chance he will."

"He knows somebody's screwing with him. What if he doesn't take the bait and just buys it on some street corner from now on?"

"No, he's more pro-active than that," Scott said. He could have divorced his wife, but he chose to do her in. He'll do something more aggressive."

"Like what?"

"I don't know. He could easily get the Denver paper online. And he'll probably start moving the accounts around to shake us off. And now that the money is in Mexico it may not be as easy for Hope to keep track of it. We may have to use other tactics. Or maybe start all over."

"I guess messing with his accounts wasn't such a good idea after all. We've given him incentive to bury his activities much deeper now."

"Well, it's all we had, Jules. Now I'm hoping something else will turn up."

"Call Scraper."

Scott hesitated. "Uuuhh."

"Call him, Scott."

"I kinda promised to keep him in the loop. And I kinda didn't. He's going to be pissed."

"Well, I kinda *did* keep him in the loop, so he won't be upset—call him."

Nick answered on the first ring. "Hey, Jules, how's Scott doing down there?"

"Hey, Nick. I'm not down there anymore."

Nick tapped his pencil on the desk for a second. "What did you get? Anything?"

"A suntan on my left elbow."

148

"Next time keep your arm in the car." Nick smiled. "Meet me at the deli in an hour. We need some face time."

Scott could tell Nick very little when they met. Nick fiddled with his coffee spoon. "So you found out where his bank account was. And then you sat in front of the bank for almost three weeks waiting for him to show up . . . that's it?"

"Of course."

"Not." Nick finished Scott's sentence.

"Well . . ."

"And if you tell me any more I'll probably have to arrest you." Nick rubbed his forehead in frustration. "Jesus! I knew this was a bad idea."

"What's happening up in Alaska?"

"Nothing." Nick shook his head. "The cruise line is four-weeks-out past your flapdoodle. It's ancient history. And the body is unclaimed. She'll be listed as a Jane Doe—drowned."

"Flapdoodle?"

"Come on, Scott."

"Well, what about the weights?"

"Never found. Probably lost as she bounced along the bottom—if they were ever there. What about your gang member? How much trouble is that going to cause me? Am I going to have to deal with the State Department at some point?"

"He was only a gang member as a kid. He got out when he was sixteen. Now he works in the law firm that Julia's law firm did business with down there. He's a very smart kid. He actually helped us figure out what bank to watch. He had a lot of experience with bankers and crooked politicians and assorted drug dealers down there."

Nick looked relieved. "Good. Don't tell me his name. I don't want to have to have him arrested for helping you."

"Did you know that in numbered bank accounts the first three numbers are . . ."

"Tut, tut, tut. I don't want to hear it, Scott."

"Okay, Nick. Moving on. This Mr. Fellows has disappeared. The only reason anybody disappears is to hide from the consequences of their actions."

"Or to get away from you."

"Come on, Nick."

"Okay, okay. *Maybe* he's disappeared for some sinister reason. But without a shred of evidence of wrongdoing I can't go after him. We still have the same rules we had when we first met, Scott. You may have bent the hell out of them a few times but they're still there."

"Fine. He's a missing person," Scott said. "I'd like to report a missing person, Agent Scraper."

"Forget it, Scott. A relative or someone who actually knows him needs to report it—like a business partner. What else you got?"

"Right now I got nothing. But I'm not letting go of this, Nick. That bastard killed his wife and was very rude to me."

"Rudeness—that bastard."

"Right. And I'm going to prove he killed his wife. If you'll remember, I was the only one who knew Mrs. Bendouski was murdered. And I helped you catch Tony Bendouski."

"I know, I know. I remember the Bendouski case. That's the only reason I'm letting you run with this, dammit," Nick sighed. "And you have to keep me in the loop on anything you do, okay?" He started to take a sip of his coffee and stopped. "Check that—keep me in the loop on anything you do that's legal." Nick got up. "I have to get back."

"That's okay, I'll get these, Nick." Scott circled his finger over the two coffees, "You'll get the next ones." But Nick was already gone.

Scott called Julia. "Hey, Jules. I met with Nick. He's got nothing, and I'm out of ideas. I'll be home in a bit. I'm going to swing by my office, check in with Clair, and then drive around downtown for a while. I need to take a few photos. You know, to clear my head a little."

"As long as you're downtown, why don't you check in on your dad as well?"

"That was the plan. See you soon." He went to his office first. "Hey, Clair. Anything?"

"Hey, Scott. The school called again to thank you for helping them. Are you still chasing the guy who drowned his wife?"

"Yes. And I don't know where it's going to take me, so why don't you just come in for half-days until I'm back?"

"Ten to two—got it. Also you're out of coffee."

"Thanks. Buy some and take it out of petty cash. Keep up the good work." Scott left and drove to the soup kitchen where his father worked. No one had seen or heard from him since the wedding. "Dammit." He photographed the homeless men in

151

the soup line, checked the streets and alleys for a few blocks in every direction, left with a heavy heart, and headed home.

~~~~~~~~~~~~~

Jason found a dealer who wasn't really fond of the rules, bought a gun, went to the Internet, and looked up Private Investigator Scott Moss. "I know it's you, you meddling son of a bitch." It took a third of a second to get Scott's office address. " There you are you bastard. You don't know who you're messing with."

~~~~~~~~~~~~~

"Dad's on a bender," Scott said when he got home. "I checked the soup kitchen. No one's seen him for a month. I'm not too surprised. He had that certain look in his eye at our wedding."

Julia sank into a chair. Words failed her.

"Did Hope find anything?" Scott asked, quickly changing the subject. He pulled the bottle of vodka from the freezer.

"She hasn't emailed anything yet," Julia said, "I hope your dad's okay."

"What are we missing here?" Scott poured a drink and went to his computer to scour through Jason Fellows's files. "Where did you screw up, Jason. Who did you call? What did you buy? Where did you go? What the hell am I *not* seeing?" Scott looked back as far as Hope Diamond was able to track Jason's phone calls. He studied the area codes. "Okay, you called Alaska a bunch of times. You called Florida a bunch of times. That takes care of the cruise and storage. Who else? One, two, three, four, five calls to New York." Scott paused. "Big city, easy to get lost? Or maybe business calls." He kept looking. He ran his finger past a 619 area code and kept looking. He suddenly stopped. "619? Okay, where's that? He made one call six months ago. But why only one call to that area?" He scanned the screen. "Only one call, and that's all. Let's see who you called in San Diego?" Scott picked up the phone and dialed.

"San Diego Realty. This is Jennifer," the very pleasant voice answered. "How can I help you?"

"Yeah, this is Jason Fellows. I was just calling to follow up on our conversation from six months ago. The deal I was thinking about . . . near that . . . you know. The thing we . . . do you remember?"

After a hesitation, he heard, "I'll have to check my notes. What was it about, again?"

"Well, it wasn't about a ham sandwich. The real estate deal, of course." Scott could hear frantic paper rustling in the background. And then frantic keyboard clicks.

"I'm sorry, I can't seem to find you, Mr. Fellows. Do you remember the property?"

"Not really. Try my partner's name. Mr. Butane. He had the point on this one. I'm pretty sure it was just a one-unit deal."

More clicking. "Oh, boy. I'm sorry, I can't find him either. You say it was one unit—six months ago. Was it a rental? Or maybe a lease? I can try to cross-check the files that way."

"Never mind. My partner just pulled in. I'll ask him and get back to you." Scott hung up. "He made one call. You can't buy, rent, or lease, with just one phone call. And you'd want to see the property."

Julia was working, but half-listening. "Did Fellows ever fly to san Diego?"

"If he did, it doesn't show up in his records. The flight to Alaska is here. And two flights to New York. Probably business. But there's nothing on a trip to San Diego." Scott paused. "Unless . . ."

". . . He didn't want it to be discovered." Julia stopped working and finished the thought.

"He's good."

"And thorough."

"But he screwed up. He only made one phone call to San Diego. Two or three, and I might have thought it was business." Scott Googled the San Diego Realty address Jason had called. "Do you feel like a long weekend in San Diego, Jules?"

"Do I *look* like a long weekend in San Diego, Scott?" Julia went back to her work. But she was wearing half a smile.

"I'll take that as a no." He went to the bedroom.

"How many days have we spent together since we got married, Scott?" Julia was matter of fact. She kept on working.

"Counting our honeymoon?" Scott was packing. "Or just the days in our apartment?" He counted on his fingers, looked at only three, and grimaced.

"Wasn't a honeymoon." Julia called out.

"Well yeah, but it started out as . . ."

"We agreed that Alaska wasn't our honeymoon. And neither was Mexico City. You owe me a real honeymoon. How many days, Scott? You and I, here, together, in our own little love shack."

"Three?"

Julia finally laughed. "Good God. You don't even know how many nights we've spent together since our wedding."

Scott made a quick mental calculation. "Well, actually, we've spent seven hundred and eighty-six nights, here, together, if you count the days on both sides of our wedding day," he said.

Now Julia stopped working completely. "No way. You made that up."

Scott's answer was a smile. He knew she'd try to figure it out. By the time he packed an overnight bag, she had a number.

"So? How many days?" he asked. "I know you counted back."

"Well of course I did, Scott. And I don't know how you did it, but you were only three days off." Julia grudgingly said.

"By your reckoning. I don't count those three days where we had that . . . thing."

"I don't remember . . ." Julia almost bought it. "What thing? We didn't . . . oh, baloney. That was just a lucky guess."

Scott wiggle-waggled his hand. "Well, just because you don't remember that place where we had that thing . . . that one time . . . doesn't mean we don't count those days."

"Goodbye, Scott. Have a nice drive to San Diego." Julia went back to her reading. "Call me," she called out as the door closed."

~~~~~~~~~~~

As Scott was driving down to San Diego on the freeway, Jackson Bellows was driving up to Los Angeles on the same freeway. The red Mustang and the big black Cadillac flew past each other at a closing speed of about 140 miles per hour, somewhere near San Clemente. Neither noticed.

~~~~~~~~~~~

Jennifer, the nice lady at San Diego Realty, couldn't find any record of a Mr. Fellows or a Mr. Butane. "I'm really sorry, Mr. Moss, I've checked everything. Neither one of them is in our records, anywhere. What did you say it was about?"

"There's a stock distribution settlement from his business. He just retired and they want to get him off their books. Apparently he was forced into retirement and he won't communicate with his old firm." Scott showed her the picture of Butane that he took on the boat. "Are you sure? Maybe his photo will jog your memory. They want to give him his money and be done with him." Scott handed her his card. "I've been retained to find him so they can finalize his distributions. They don't want him to come back later and sue them. I guess he's a real killer when it comes to money."

The gal smiled. "I know him. That's Jackson Bellows. You got the name wrong. No wonder I couldn't find him. He leased a house on the beach from us a few months ago. He certainly didn't seem poor. The house he leased is quite a place."

"Yeah, well, rich people can never have enough, I guess. Can I have the address, please?"

"I better call him first." She picked up the phone. "Just to make sure it's all right."

Scott smiled. "Absolutely. Give him a call. Tell him it's about the money he left in his account."

"His account?"

"Yeah, the final whatever they call it. The retirement distribution account, thing. I don't know what they call it. I'm just supposed to locate him so they can send him the money. Apparently they're as sick of him as he is of them."

"So you said." The gal dialed. "It went to the answering machine. Mr. Bellows, this is Jennifer, at San Diego Realty. There's a Mr. Moss here, who would like to speak with you . . ."

"Tell him it's about the money he left behind. Rich people always want every cent they think they deserve." Scott winked.

". . . about a financial matter. Please give us a call when you can. Thank you." Jennifer hung up. "I'm sorry, Mr. Moss. I left the message. That's about all I can do."

Scott had been reading her notes upside down. "That's okay, Jennifer. I'll come back later." He wrote the street number down as he left. "Okay, Mr. Bellows. How do we play this little game?

Direct confrontation? Scare tactics?" Scott hummed thoughtfully. "You probably don't scare easily. Lets see what happens if we meet face on face one more time." He headed for the address.

~~~~~~~~~~~

Jackson Bellows found Scott's office. He sat in the parking lot, fiddling with his gun. Finally he said, "Okay, Mr. Moss, Let's see what you're made of." He checked his pistol one last time, went to Scott's office, took a breath, and opened the door.

Clair smiled and put her paperback in a drawer. "How can I help you?"

Jackson twitched. He wasn't expecting to deal with a witness. "I, uhh . . . never mind," he said, and quickly retreated.

Clair recognized him. "Uh-oh." She grabbed the phone and dialed. "Scott that guy was just here—the guy in the photo. Where are you?"

Scott was standing in Jackson Bellows's living room. "I'm in his house. Dammit! Is he still there? What did he say?"

"He said, 'Never mind' and left. I'm going home, Scott. He could have had a gun."

"I'm so sorry, Clair. Get out of there right away." He called Nick Scraper. "Nick, the killer was just in my office and I'm worried he'll show up at my apartment next. Julia is working there, and she's all by herself."

Nick was already out of his chair. "I'll meet you there. How close are you?"

158

"I'm in *his* house in San Diego!"

"Jesus! Call Jules. Tell her to get out right now. Have her go to her office or somewhere safe. I'll get to your place as fast as I can." Nick was running down the hall. "What the hell are you doing down there? And how the hell were you able you find out where he lives?"

"Unimportant detail. I gotta call Jules." Scott hung up and called.

"Hey, Scott. What's up?" Julia was sitting on the couch with her usual pile of briefs.

"Get out of the apartment, Jules. That bastard, Fellows, may be on his way there right now."

"But how . . ."

"Just go!" he screamed and flew out Bellows's front door, leaving it wide open. He backed his Mustang down the driveway and headed up the street just as the police came tearing up the street the other way. He called again. "Are you out?" he screamed into the phone.

"I had to put away some papers. I'm just getting my purse, now," she said.

"Jules! Leave everything and get out of there, right now!" Scott thought for a moment. "Nick is on his way. Leave the door unlocked."

"Why?"

"Just do it!" Scott hung up. He was panicked.

Julia got into her car and, as she was about to leave, Fellows showed up in his big black Cadillac. "Uh-oh." She slumped down, watched him park, check the address, and slip inside. She called Scott. "He just showed up and went inside."

"Did he see you?"

"No, he didn't. I was already in my car and I ducked down. He couldn't have seen me."

"Nick is on the way. Sit tight."

"Where are you?"

"I'm back on the freeway." Scott was flying. "I'll be there as quick as I can. Don't do anything until Nick gets there." Scott hung up and called Nick. "Nick, Jules is out. I told her to leave the door unlocked. You just might catch him inside."

"Is he armed?"

"No idea, but probably yes."

Before Nick could get there, Bellows got a phone call from the police in San Diego. His house had been broken into. It looked like nothing was taken. Bellows was standing in Scott and Julia's living room, very shaken. "Thank you, Officer. I'll be home as soon as I can. Please close the door for me. Thank you." Jackson looked around, looked at the unlocked door, yelled, "You bastard! You set me up!" and ran out of the apartment.

Julia watched him run to his car. "Come on, Nick, where are you?" The Cadillac raced away as Julia started her Buick. "Ohh, boy. This isn't very smart." She called Nick. "Nick, he got here and left in a big hurry. I'm following him."

"Ahh, dammit, Jules! I'm almost there. Don't do anything rash. Can you see his license plate?"

"I'm two cars back. That's what you do, right?"

"Ahh, Jesus. Lay your phone on the seat, Jules, and recite the streets you're driving on. Talk loud. I'll try to find you while you're moving."

"Loudly," she mumbled.

Scott was racing up the freeway.

Julia was dutifully bellowing out the streets and following Bellows.

Nick was trying to figure out how to intercept a moving target.

Traffic suddenly backed up. Bellows stopped abruptly, and the car behind him rear-ended his Cadillac. Julia almost ran into the car behind the car that rammed the Cadillac. The car behind Julia managed to stop. Julia sat, stuck behind the wreck. "Ohh, this isn't good."

Bellows was out, exchanging cards with the driver of the car that rammed him. The car behind them and in front of Julia started laying on his horn. "Come on, come on, move it off to the side. It's just a fender-bender for God's sake."

Bellows looked back. Julia was watching. She couldn't duck her head back inside quick enough.

He swore, she gulped, and he walked directly toward her car. Julia hit the door locks and powered up the windows. He ran up and pounded on her window as she pulled out of traffic and made a U-turn. "Nick! He saw me!" she screamed, while he pounded on her window. "He's at my car. I have to get away from here."

"I'm almost there, Jules. Hang on!"

Bellows ran back to his car, shoved the guy who hit him out of the way, and raced after Julia.

"Nick, he's chasing me!" she screamed.

"Hang on!" he screamed back.

Traffic going away from the fender-bender was light. Traffic going toward it was heavy. Nick was stuck. He watched Julia race past him. "Jules! You just passed me. Pull over."

"He's after me, Nick." Julia said in a panic.

"I'm right here. Pull over!" Nick turned on his lights, put a flasher on his roof, hit his siren, and started turning around. He pushed the car in front of him out of the way, to the outrage of that driver, and jockeyed his car out of traffic.

Julia had stopped. Nick made a U-turn, pulled up behind her, and looked back. "I don't see him."

"He's in a black Cadillac, Nick."

Bellows got off the gas when he saw the flashing lights. He turned one block before he got to Nick's car and disappeared down a side street.

Julia's phone rang. She started to answer but Nick took it from her. "She's safe."

"Oh God, Nick. I love you." Scott slowed to the speed limit. "Did you get Bellows—Fellows?"

Nick was looking up the street. "Julia said he was coming this way but he must have turned off. Dammit! I shouldn't have used my lights."

"He was in a fender-bender," Julia said. "I saw them exchange cards."

"Scott, I gotta go. Julia, you stay here." Nick hit his lights and siren again and headed back to the accident corner. Crushed glass in the street was all that was left. "Dammit!"

Julia pulled up behind him.

"You were supposed to stay put."

"Uh-huh. I'll stay put right next to you if you don't mind." She looked up and down the street. "That man gives me the creeps."

"Well, we know his car is banged up. We know where he lives. He shouldn't be too hard to find."

"Hey, Nick. Did you forget that he has over eight million dollars, in a numbered account, in another country," Julia asked.

Nick closed his eyes. "I take it back," he said. "He'll be very hard to find."

Scott was cruising at the speed limit when he saw flashing lights racing up behind him. "Uh-oh." He slowed and pulled into the right lane. "Drive on past. Come on, drive on past."

The police car pulled up behind him and hit the siren. "Crap!" Scott pulled over, got out his driver's license, his detective license, and put Nick's phone number on a piece of paper from his note pad. "This'll be fun." He powered down the window as the officer walked up.

"I'm surprised you slowed down," the officer angrily said. "You shot past us so fast I thought we might never catch you."

Scott handed him the two licenses and the piece of paper. "That's who I am and that's the phone number of FBI Agent Nick Scraper. My wife was in serious danger. I was speeding to . . ."

The officer held up his hand. "Stop talking. You could have killed a dozen people the speed you were driving." He studied the license, Scott's detective license, and the phone number. "Is this

163

supposed to give you the right to endanger every driver on the freeway?"

"No, that was wrong. But please call Agent Scraper, Officer—please."

"Stay put." The officer went back to his car.

Scott watched in his rearview mirror as the officer made calls. Ten minutes passed and Scott said, "Ohh, this isn't going to end well."

The cop finally returned. "Sign here," he said and shoved the ticket in through the window.

Scott read the ticket. It was for driving too fast for conditions. "Oh, wow, did you . . ."

"Don't say another word, Mr. Moss. The only reason I'm not arresting you and tossing you in a jail cell, is because Special Agent Scraper explained the situation and vouched for you. Your wife is safe. Just sign the damn ticket and drive home safely."

"Yes, sir." Scott signed. "Thank you, Officer."

"Have a nice fricken day." The cop gave Scott his copy and stormed back to his patrol car.

Scott tossed the ticket on the passenger seat and moved on. "And thank you, Special Agent Nick Scraper," he said to himself.

Chapter 11
A Person of Interest

Jason Fellows drove to a luxury hotel on Sunset Boulevard, checked in, without luggage, as Jackson Bellows, and went to his room. He paced for a while, sat for a while, and paced some more. "Son of a bitch," he mumbled.

He sat on the edge of the bed and fiddled with his pistol for a while, and then suddenly surged out of the room.

~~~~~~~~~~~~

By the time Scott got home, Julia was back at their apartment. He used his key and opened the door to find Julia standing, defiantly, holding a big kitchen carving knife.

"Whoa. Are you okay?" he asked.

"I've been better," she sighed. "That creep scared the business out of me." Then she wrapped her arms around him. "I'm glad you're finally home. I've been a little tense waiting for you."

"I can see that," Scott gently said.

"I really felt alone, Scott. I guess I didn't realize how much I depend on you."

"I'm here now. You're okay." He kept an eye on the knife in Julia's hand, her arm wrapped all the way around his neck put the sharp edge of the blade right in front of his face. He tried not to flinch. "You're okay now."

As she pulled away, he gently took her hand and guided the blade away from them. "Catch me up. What's happening?"

"Nick's opened an official case. That's the one good thing about all this, I guess."

"Okay, great." Scott took the kitchen knife from Julia's hand and put it back in the kitchen. "What made him change his mind?"

"The FBI called all the insurance companies and traced the guy who rear-ended Fellows. Fellows gave him a card that said Jerald Butane. It was just enough to make a connection to the alleged incident on the boat in Alaska."

"He gave the captain a business card?"

"I don't think so. They had the name on the passenger list. There's no proof of a murder or anything, but at least they have a legitimate reason to question him—if they can find him. The San Diego FBI agents are sitting on his house now. But Nick says he probably won't go back there. He leased the house under the name Jackson Bellows."

"Yeah. I found that out in San Diego."

"So, what do you want to do now? Nick's on the case. He's got all the means we don't have to find Fellows. Can we leave it to him?"

"He doesn't have the numbered accounts. I can give him those."

"But you acquired them illegally. Nick probably won't be able to use them to find Fellows. He probably won't even be able to get permission to track the numbers down. Fellows is just a person of interest. They'll talk to him like the Alaska Troopers did. He can make up any story he wants."

Scott gave Julia a frustrated stare. "You had to be a *good* lawyer, didn't you?"

"It saves a lot of time. And I'm way better than just good."

"How do we help Nick, help us?"

"Wait a minute." Julia turned on her computer. "Give me the numbers, Scott."

"You just said if you give them to Nick, he still has to get a court order."

"Yes, but with the account numbers he'll be able to work backward. He should be able to find Fellows-Butane-Bellows in hours instead of weeks. The court doesn't need to know *how* the FBI found him. Once they have him, the account numbers are irrelevant. The court's not going to care how they found him. The money doesn't matter anyway—the murder does."

"So they find him, they question him. He's done very weird things with his money, which apparently is irrelevant. And there's no proof he's involved in a crime. What are we doing?"

"Well, he had a wife, Scott. Where is she? If he still has the new wife, the old wife's friends will testify that she's not her."

"That's right. But, I'm betting he's alone," Scott said. "That should be enough to convict him. He'll have to explain why she's not there. Or anywhere."

"Circumstantial. She left him—she hates him. He can't find her, he's distraught. Any good lawyer would use that as a defense."

"Maybe he'll get a crappy lawyer."

"Yeah, right. Eight million dollars buys a boatload of awfully good lawyers, Scott. He'll hire an army of legal eagles if he has to."

"Ohh. He's good."

"He's very good."

"We have to trick him," Scott said.

"We have to find him first."

"So, we'll find him—with the help of our friends at the FBI—and then we'll trick him. Scott slapped the numbers on Julia's desk. "Go get 'em, Sherlock." He watched Julia's fingers fly across the keys. "After that we can get something to eat."

Julia sent the information to Nick, along with her work-backwards suggestion. "Okay. Let's eat."

While Mr. and Mrs. Scott Moss were quietly eating at SushiMas, Mr. Jackson Bellows was frantically trying to move his millions to new numbered accounts on a newly purchased laptop. His own security was giving him fits. It wouldn't recognize his new computer.

And Agent Nick Scraper was getting the proper authority to go after Jason Fellows, aka Jerald Butane, aka Jackson Bellows. He literally had to wake up a judge.

The judge was pissed, but Nick got his warrant.

Chapter 12
He's Not Going Anywhere

Frustrated and furious at his inability to move his accounts remotely, Jason Fellows took off for the airport. He would fly to Mexico City on his real passport, and change the accounts in person.

The FBI missed his exit from the United States by a few hours. And, as he was only a "person of interest" at that point, they would have to wait for his return to question him.

Nick called Scott. "Your man, Fellows, flew down to Mexico yesterday, Scott. We'll pick him up for questioning when he returns."

"*If* he returns, Nick. He's had two very close calls. I wouldn't come back if I were in his shoes. What about his money?"

Julia was listening. "Irrelevant," she said.

"Irrelevant," Nick echoed.

Scott smacked his desk. "How can eight million dollars of a killer's money be irrelevant?"

"The money might have helped us find him, but now that we know where he is—it's more or less irrelevant." Nick was enjoying Scott's frustration.

"How can eight million dollars be irrelevant? It has to fit in this business somewhere."

"It's just his money, Scott," Julia said. Then she stopped. "It is a motive, though, if they were having marriage troubles. And a wife in a wheelchair, for the whatever-it-was that put her there, could easily put a strain on a marriage."

"You're right. With her gone, he wouldn't have to give her half his fortune in a divorce." Scott went back to Fellows's files. "Let's see if he ever called a divorce lawyer?"

"Hey, Scott?" Nick was still on the line.

"Yeah, Nick?"

"I like where you're going. But off the record and completely unofficial of course. Let's have coffee in a couple of days."

"You got it, Nick. As soon as I get back from Denver." Scott hung up and printed out all of Jason's files—including phone numbers called.

"What did Nick just say?" Julia asked.

"He tacitly said it was okay to dig deeper into Fellows's personal life."

"*Tacitly* said it was okay?" Julia smiled. "You two do have a way."

Nick looked at his phone and shook his head. "This better work." Then he hung up.

"Do you feel like a trip to Denver, Jules?"

Julia was working at her desk. She never looked up from her computer. "Do I look like . . ."

"Don't say it!" Scott went to the bedroom to pack. "Okay, Jules, you can add a few more days we aren't staying together in our place."

170

"How nice for us." Julia called, and went back to work. "We were together more when we weren't married," she mumbled.

"I heard that!" Scott was stuffing his suitcase, suppressing a laugh.

"Well, its true, isn't it?" Julia waited for a retort but Scott didn't answer.

~~~~~~~~~~

Jason Fellows spent the next two and a half days in Mexico City rearranging his accounts. Splitting the money up tripled the work. So he decided to put all his bucks in one bucket. Then he spent another day trying to figure out where to live. San Diego was out, along with his lease deposit. It was too boring anyway. Florida was out—too close to his old furniture. Chicago was too cold and the Bears were certainly no prize. He decided to try New Orleans. He'd have to root for the Saints, plus live through Mardi Gras—but they had much better bars. He fired up his new computer and started looking for a house.

~~~~~~~~~~

Scott's trip to Denver was optimistic, finding friends of Mr. or Mrs. Fellows was tricky. Plus his old law firm had dissolved so there was no easy way to trace Jason's clients. Scott settled on the printout of Fellows's phone numbers. He would call, and if a man answered he would hang up. If a

171

woman answered, he would ask about Joyce Fellows. After a few phone calls he was able to piece together her story. She had been in a car accident that broke her back. She would be in a wheelchair for the rest of her life. But it was her fault—negligence—many people were injured, and Jason and Joyce were being sued by them all—for a lot of money. As the lawsuits started piling up Jason realized they were way underinsured. He knew he would be stuck with a huge financial burden. So, a month after Joyce got out of the hospital, they both disappeared.

"Finally, something to identify Mrs. Joyce Fellows." Scott called Nick. "Hey, Nick, the real Mrs. Fellows had a broken back. She ran a red light at sixty, and hit two other cars. Lots of people were badly hurt."

"And that means . . . what, Scott?"

"It means she couldn't have gotten out of her wheelchair. Jules and I, and half the people on the boat saw her get out of it to sit down and eat. And she was seen walking around, shopping. You've got a case. If the Jane Doe up in Alaska has a broken back, it's a slam-dunk. She was wrapped around a rock in the river but I'm reasonably certain they can tell old wounds from new wounds. So, Nick, you'll have the proof you need."

"Did you get the name of the hospital?"

"No. Not yet, but . . ."

"Never mind. We can find it. The hospital will have X-rays. We'll check the body for a match. I'll call Alaska. They can X-ray the Jane Doe while

172

we're finding the hospital." Nick said. "Not bad Scott. You may have identified a Jane Doe and exposed a killer."

"Thanks, Nick."

Nick sat, tapping his pencil on his little pad for a moment. "Hey, Scott, how long have you been in Denver anyway?"

"Got here this morning. Why?"

Nick shook his head at Scott's speed. "I was just wondering if you broke your own record. I'll call Alaska—keep in touch." Nick hung up, stared at the phone for a moment, and then muttered to himself, "You're a really helpful pain in the ass, aren't you?"

Scott was staring at his phone. "Where are you now, Jason? And what are you going to do next?" Scott smiled. "Follow the money."

~~~~~~~~~~~

Jason loaded up two money belts, flew from Mexico to Vancouver, Canada, under his own name and rode a bus back into the United States. He hotwired an old car in Bellingham, Washington, and drove it down to Seattle. He abandoned the car at the Seattle-Tacoma Airport and flew to San Francisco under the name Jackson Bellows. He used the name J. W. Butane to fly to Dallas. From there, he planned to search the local ads, test drive a car from a private seller, never return, and drive it to New Orleans. He had saved one last name and ID to settle down under. Jack Jackson.

J. J. would buy or lease a place in or near the Garden District and settle down to live a quiet life—free of lawsuits, wheel-chaired wives, and murder charges. That was his plan.

But once in Dallas he started worrying about those two irritatingly nosy people—the Mosses. He woke up in his hotel room, in the middle of the night, his gut twisting. He poured himself a drink and sat, staring out the window. Could he leave those two loose ends dangling? Could he risk it? He poured another drink. "Shit!"

~~~~~~~~~~

Scott decided there was nothing more to gain by staying in Denver, so he headed back to Los Angeles. He called Hope from the Denver Airport to have her check on Jason's numbered accounts.

She looked for them, but the accounts had vanished. "They're all gone, Scott."

Scott yelled, "All of them?"

"Yep," she said. "He must have moved the money to some other accounts."

"*All* the money?" He yelled so loud that the people at the gate all stopped and stared. He pointed to his cell phone. "Honey! We lost all the honey. Our beehives were attacked by a bear."

"What bear? What honey?" Hope was still on the phone.

"I'll call you when I get back. Thanks, Hope."

"What honey, Scott?" she asked.

Scott hung up without answering.

Hope looked at her phone. "He's crazier than a monkey on crack."

Scott boarded, got seated, and called Julia from the plane. "Hey, Jules. I'm headed home. We're just about to take off."

"Hey, Scott. Did you get what you were after?"

"Oh yeah. I got enough to get Nick a conviction. But Hope says we've lost the money trail. Fellows moved the money, just like we thought he would. Probably to another numbered account or two—or three."

"So, what are you thinking? Can Hope find them if she keeps looking?"

"She's trying, but she didn't seem to think so. I'm thinking one of Izzy's questionable banking connections down in Mexico might help us pick up the trail again."

"Whoa, Scott. His connections sounded a lot like the Mexican Mafia? You can't do that, you'll get Izzy killed."

"Izzy won't get killed. And we don't know for sure that they're Mafia." His seat partner perked up, while Scott continued, "They could just play fast and loose with their decimal points and stuff."

"And stuff?" Julia slowly shook her head.

"They're probably just politicians. Politicians in most countries don't like negative publicity." Scott winked at his seatmate. "He'll be fine."

Julia was still on the line. "All the same, you better be careful who you're messing with down there. Those guys play for keeps."

"With whom I'm messing." Scott checked his watch. "Can you pick me up? My plane lands in an hour and forty-five minutes."

"Touché. What airline?"

"United."

"Okay, but it's not your plane, it belongs to United. I'll see you at the curb." Julia hung up smiling. "Well . . . it's never dull."

Scott hung up and stared at his phone. "We don't know it's their plane. Maybe it's leased. And I love you too." Scott called Clair. "Hey, Clair. I'll be in some time tomorrow."

Scott's seat partner was still staring at him. "I'm not usually this vociferous," Scott said, "And technically, we're still on our honeymoon."

"Are you with the FBI?" he asked.

"Actually, no. I'm just a private citizen. But a guy killed his wife, pissed me off, and screwed up our honeymoon. So, now I'm hunting him down."

"Uh-huh." His seatmate leaned away from him.

~~~~~~~~~~

"Hope called," Julia said, as Scott got in her car.

"And?"

"And she's still not getting anywhere. Fellows has managed to bury his trail completely."

"Plan B." Scott got on the phone. "Izzy! Scott Moss—up in the States. How are you?"

"Ohh, this'll be fun," Julia said.

"Hey, Izzy. How hard would it be for one of your banking friends to trace a numbered account?"

"Five bucks says it's not hard at all," Julia said.

Scott smiled as he listened. "Okay. But I'll have to check and get back to you tomorrow." He hung up and dug out a five.

Julia snatched it from his hand, but kept her eyes on the road. "What'd he say?"

"What you said, word for word. But he said it might cost some serious dollars."

"Uh-oh. We're not paying for this out of our own pockets, Scott. Especially since you're not earning any money right now."

"No, no, no." Scott stared out the side window. "So, how can we get the FBI to pay without them knowing what they're paying for?"

"They have a fund for informants, don't they? Try that for starters."

"That's why you get the big bucks." Scott called Nick. "Hey, Nick, what have you found out?"

"Jane Doe is Joyce Fellows. Nice work, Scott. Fellows is already on our most wanted list."

Outstanding. And I can get some really good information on him, but I have to pay for it."

Nick started tapping his pencil on his pad. Finally he said, "An informant. Okay. But I'll have to have a name. And I can't pay anyone to do anything illegal, Scott."

"Nick! Would I ever . . ."

"Don't! Don't say anything. Just tell me the name and what we might get for our money."

"His name is Hector Israel. And we'll get a lead on where Mr. Jason Fellows is hiding out."

"Hector Israel. What the hell kind of stupid name is that, Scott? You're not trying to pull a fake-out on me, are you?"

"No. I'm trying to get you some information on Fellows without *you* breaking the law."

"Without me . . . ahh, Jesus. I'll probably end up in a cell right next to that bastard."

"Not a chance, Nick. It's all on me."

"Yeah right." Nick tossed his pencil on the desk. "How much?"

"I won't know how much until tomorrow. I'll call you then—with an amount." Scott heard a click. "Nice talking to you, Nick."

Julia smiled. "He hung up on you, didn't he?"

"Yeah, well, he's not real happy. But it sounds like he's going to get us the money."

Nick got on the phone to Washington. "This is going to be painful."

~~~~~~~~~~

Jason Fellows had spent a few sleepless nights in Dallas before he decided he *had* to go back to LA. He would "end" the Mosses and get back to his plan. His biggest problem was, he'd run out of fake names. He hadn't counted on needing more than three IDs to vanish. He didn't want to use Jack Jackson—that was his end-game name. He could take the train. They didn't require a name, did they? He could hire a private plane. As long as the right pilot got the right amount of money, he wouldn't care, would he? Fellows decided to check his new

178

numbered account while he stewed about how to get back to Los Angeles. The money was there and accessible from his new computer. Relieved, he decided to have a few drinks in a respectable bar somewhere nearby.

LA could wait a day.

Scott waited, impatiently, to hear from Izzy. "I hope your contacts are reasonable, Izzy. Nick won't like it if we try to jack it up too high."

~~~~~~~~~~~

Izzy contacted a questionable moneyman from his teenage gang days. The information would only cost fifteen hundred American. A small favor for an old associate.

Scott was delighted; he thought it was a bargain. Nick thought it was highway robbery. "Good God, Scott, the most our informants get is around one or two hundred bucks for any tip."

"Come on, Nick, it's very reasonable."

"I can't shell out fifteen hundred dollars. How's that going to look in an official report?"

"Hell I don't know. When you catch the killer is anybody going to care?"

"Hell yes, they're going to care! And there's no guarantee we're going to catch the bastard with your information." Nick held his head.

Scott listened to silence for about a minute and finally asked, "Nick, are you still there?"

"Yeah, I'm still here. Look. Go ahead with the plan. I'll try to figure out how to get you the money

179

in installments. And if I end up in prison for this, I'm taking you with me, dammit!" Nick slammed the phone down. When he looked up, Jim, his number-two guy, was standing in his doorway. What?" he barked.

"Nothing." Jim cringed as he slipped away.

Scott smiled and gently set the phone down. "Nick's really pissed."

"No surprise there," Julia said, not looking up from her work.

"Jules, I'm going to front the money and Nick is going to pay us back in installments. That's okay with you isn't it?"

"Gee, I don't know, Scott. Do you think the FBI is good for it?" Julia was hiding her smile.

"I'll take that as a yes." Scott got on the phone. "Izzy. It's a go. Yeah, that's American slang for you got the money. But don't send the numbers by email. Better call and give them to me over the phone. How long? Okay, great. Yes I can wire the money to you, but after I get the number. Of course I trust *you*, Izzy, but I don't know the man you're working with. Well, he can't be that honest, he's breaking the law for us, right?" Scott waited. "Sorry, that's the deal." Scott waited for Izzy to make up his mind. After a moment he nodded. "Okay, good. I'll talk to you in a couple of days."

"You don't trust Izzy," Julia said, flatly, never looking up from her work.

"Hell no," Scott said, chuckling.

~~~~~~~~~~

Jason called his Mexico bank and had all his millions converted to bond certificates, held for a day, and then re-deposited into another numbered account—but in a different branch of the same bank—effectively breaking the chain. The banks naturally assumed it was a drug-related transfer and didn't say a word—to anybody.

Nick Scraper had all he needed to go after Jason Fellows. The FBI went after his accounts, but with the recent break in the transfer chain it would be close to impossible to trace them.

Izzy's darkly connected friend had a head start, but even he was having a difficult time. The banks involved were afraid to reveal anything, lest it be to the wrong gang.

Scott was encouraging Hope, but she was at a loss as well. "I don't know what else to do, Scott. He made the money disappear. It goes from one account to a total withdrawal. Then nothing."

"Well, we had him for a little while, didn't we? Thanks for the help, kiddo. I'll take it from here." Scott called Nick. "Hey, Nick. Have you turned up anything on your end?"

"Not yet. We think he might be in Canada. How's your informant doing?"

"Haven't heard. I'll let you know the minute I hear anything. What about that chief steward, Ron Lon Somebody?"

"McDonnell. He's disappeared as well. He could be just traveling or something, but I'd bet serious money he was in on the murder. That means he's hiding out, or maybe he got dealt with more permanently by our Mr. Fellows."

"What about the fake wife?"

"A good guess would be either on the run with Fellows, or dead. I hate saying this, but your lead in Mexico may be our one last hope, Scott."

"He's good."

"He's very good. Keep in touch." Nick hung up.

Jason Fellows was able to catch the train to LA without showing any ID. It would take almost two full days to get there, but he could safely bring a weapon in his belongings.

"You can't win 'em all, Scott." Julia sounded very sympathetic. "You know what, why don't we commiserate at SushiMas? I'll buy."

Scott smiled. "That always sounded so good when we weren't married. Now it's just . . . us." He paused. "Come to think of it, you never picked up the check when we weren't married, did you? Not that I can remember anyway. Why is that?"

"Well, you were courting me. That's the way it works. You chase me, you shower me with gifts, you take me to lavish dinners, and I finally give in and agree to marry you."

"In the last century maybe," Scott quipped, and opened the door for her. "Now it's just *our* money."

Julia gave him a sideways glance. "Maybe I should have had a pre-nup."

Scott paused. "Well . . . some months you do make more money than me."

"Some months?" Julia smiled. "And it's *than I*."

"Really?"

"Some months you make more money *than I make* is the complete thought."

"I'm just sayin'."

~~~~~~~~~~~

While Scott and Julia were having dinner at SushiMas, Jason Fellows was having drinks—way too many drinks, in the train's club car. He was on his way to Los Angeles. After a good number of martinis he was unable to stand. He sat, blurry-eyed, cursing Scott under his breath.

"Do you have a sleeping car, Sir?" the porter asked. "We're closing for the night."

"Damn right, I do." Fellows tried to stand and almost fell. The porter caught him and escorted him down the aisle.

"What number, sir?"

Fellows fumbled for his key. "Here."

The porter helped him into his room and sat him on the bed. When he left, Fellows fell face-first on the blanket and never moved.

He woke up, with a blinding headache, still in his clothes. He went to his little bathroom, and threw up in the toilet. It was just daybreak and the sun suddenly stabbed through his window, blinding him. "Ahhh!" He yanked the blackout shade down and pulled it off the window." Ahhh, shit!"

Scott woke up feeling empty. "Dammit. I hate that that guy is out there, free."

Julia rolled over, still half-asleep. "Let it go, Scott. You can't win 'em all."

Fellows stood at his door holding his head, while the porter fixed his shade.

Julia made coffee, while Scott scrambled eggs and made toast. "This is nice," he said.

Fellows pulled the repaired shade down, took off his clothes and went back to bed. "This is shit," he said. "I ought to kill that bastard twice."

~~~~~~~~~~~

"Where do you suppose Fellows is hiding?"

"France? Spain? Italy? Russia?" Julia collected her things. "I have a meeting downtown. Let it go, Scott, he's gone." She was out the door.

"I wish I could." Scott sat drumming his fingers on the kitchen table. "Maybe Nick's right. He could have easily dropped into Canada and started over." Scott drummed away. "But I don't think so." He drummed some more. "He put his money in Mexico." More drumming. "But he stayed in the States." More drumming. "He leased a house in San Diego, not somewhere in Mexico." Scott continued drumming. "He murdered her in Alaska, not overseas. Why?" More drumming. "Was it because he couldn't get there without shots or something? Was it because he needed to take her someplace that wouldn't cause her to suspect anything? Maybe he doesn't like the food in Europe?" Scott suddenly sat up. "No. It's because that's where everyone would expect him to go." Scott slapped the table. "He's not going to leave the country. He's going to hide in plain sight. He's in the States and he's going to stay here." Scott called Nick. "Hey, Nick. Have you gotten any leads?"

"No. Interpol is on it. We're monitoring flights. His passport picture is being circulated . . ."

"Don't bother, Nick. He's right here in the States and he's not going to leave."

"Come on, Scott, you don't know that. He's got enough money to hide out anywhere he wants."

"He could but he won't leave for very long. He's had half a dozen chances to skip the country permanently, but he never does. And when he does leave, he comes right back again. He's right here, Nick. He's somewhere in the United States—I just know it in my bones."

"Bad movie line, Scott.' Nick hesitated. "But maybe he is. What about your snitch in Mexico?"

"Nothing yet."

"Call me if you get something." Nick hung up.

Chapter 13
I Like Clowns

Scott showed up at his office for the first time in three weeks. "Hey, Clair."

"Hey, Scott. Everybody called," Clair said.

"Again?" Scott smiled and started through a pile of pink phone slips. He stopped at the third one. "What's does this American Legion call mean? Somebody stole their bar?"

"Apparently, someone, or ones, came in and took all their booze. The door wasn't jimmied, so I told them to check everybody who came in that night with the smell of booze on their breath. They never called back, so I may have cracked the case."

"Nicely done." Scott kept sorting. "What's this call about a pink paint-job on a black Mercedes?"

"Apparently somebody hand-painted some rich guy's wife's car with a big brush. He wanted you to find the Michelangelo."

"His wife did it," Scott said flatly.

Clair paused. "Of course she did. Why didn't I think of that?"

"Is there anything interesting here, Clair?"

"The bottom one. I told the clown you might be interested in helping, but you wouldn't be able to for a couple of weeks."

"Clown? Nice talk." Scott pulled out the bottom slip. "Ohh. She really is a clown."

Clair smiled.

"Somebody stole her donkey?" Scott stared at the slip. "Why would anybody steal a donkey?"

"The donkey can count."

"Ohh? So . . . a rival clown. Make a list of all the circus acts in LA while I give this Ms. Cleopatra Calamity a call." He dialed. "Ms. Calamity? Scott Moss here. I'm sorry to call so late. Any word on your missing donkey? Okay—Cleo. Any word?"

Clair brought him a list.

Scott nodded. "Yes I can. My fee is . . ."

Clair interrupted with a loud cough.

"Hold on a sec." Scott held his hand over the mouthpiece. "What?"

"Five hundred," Clair said, sternly.

"That's half-price," Scott whispered. "Do you know her or something?"

She stabbed her finger at him.

"Fine, five hundred a day." Scott was about to tell her his rate. "Cleo, I charge five . . ."

"Total!" Clair interrupted. "Five hundred, total."

". . . hundred total, to recover a stolen donkey. That's the going rate." He threw up his hands and gave Clair a "why" look.

"I like clowns." Clair marched back to her desk.

Scott was still on the phone. "Okay, a hundred a month will be fine. I'll get right on it. No, you can start paying me *after* I find your donkey. You're very welcome." Scott hung up. "We're going to end up in the poorhouse Clair!"

"I doubt it," she mumbled.

Scott spent almost all day calling clown acts. "Hi. I'm having a party for my nephew. Do you have anything new and different? He's nine and very hard to entertain." He got what he was after on the twentieth call. "A donkey that counts? Wow, that ought to impress the little bugger. Actually, it's tomorrow. I decided I needed something different at the very last minute. Can you? Great. How much? Seven-fifty for the short notice. Ouch, that much? Okay, I guess. My secretary will give you the address." Scott covered the phone. "Clair, would you pick up. Please?"

She had been listening. "Hi. The party's in Mathew Meadow Park, at eleven o'clock. You can Google it, okay? Yes, we'll bring a check. Terrific, see you tomorrow."

Scott called Cleo. "Your donkey will be at Mathew Meadow Park at eleven o'clock tomorrow. The bad clown thinks he's entertaining at a party. No, I don't need to be there. Ask for a police car to meet you there. Sure, they'll send a car, just tell them what's happening. You're very welcome, Cleo. After you get your donkey back, my secretary will send you the bill."

Clair picked up. "The price will be two hundred and fifty dollars. Mr. Moss was able to track your donkey down much faster than we anticipated."

Scott hung up and bellowed, "Clair!"

Clair hung up and bellowed back, "Come on! You made ten phone calls. She has to feed her donkey even when he isn't working. And she has to buy gas. And do you have any idea how much a good clown costume costs? And other stuff?"

"Other stuff? Like what, rubber noses? And it was at least twenty calls, dammit."

"So? At twelve dollars and fifty cents a phone call, you still make out."

"Jeez. Never argue with a clown lover," Scott mumbled to himself.

"I heard that."

The next day Julia worked at home all morning. Scott sat and stewed. At noon he called Cleo. "Hey, it's Scott. Did you get your donkey back?"

"Yes, I did, Mr. Moss. Thank you so much. And as a bonus, Sam kicked the man who stole her. Sam was the biggest part of my routine. I never would have been able to get jobs without her."

"Your donkey's name is Sam? And she's a girl. Interesting."

"Her full name is actually Samantha Elizabeth Chelsea Bernardino. But I just call her Sam."

"Ooookay."

"Okay, what?"

"Nothing. Clair, my secretary will handle the financial arrangements. I'm glad Sam's back."

Cleo hesitated. "Mr. Moss, would it be okay if I only paid you fifty dollars a month? The clown business isn't as lucrative as you might think."

"And I'll bet Samantha eats up a lot of the profits," Scott replied.

"Ohh! That's really cute, Mr. Moss. I can use that in my act."

"Call me Scott. And you can use anything I say in your act. Plus, I'm sure Clair will be more than generous with any arrangements that you may need regarding the fee. She's a big fan—bye."

"Clair's a clown fan?" Julia smiled.

Scott shook his head and hung up. "Apparently, so. Okay, Mr. Fellows, where are you?"

"Leave him to the FBI, Scott. They'll find him eventually. And the donkey's name is Samantha?"

"Samantha Elizabeth Chelsea Bernardino."

"Good God. Does she have golden hooves?"

Scott wasn't listening. "If you were Fellows where would you go, Jules?"

"Forget Jason Fellows, and find a paying job, Scott. We've got bills to pay."

"I'm going down to my office. Maybe I'll think of something on the way."

"Well, find a paying case! Find somebody's lost aunt. And say 'hey' to Clair." Julia watched him leave and sighed. "He's never going to let it go."

~~~~~~~~~~

Scott opened his door to find Clair reading a paperback. "Hector Israel just called," she said.

"There's an overseas account number on your desk that seems to be very important."

"Outstanding! We've picked up Jason Fellow's trail again." Scott ran to his desk. "Wire Izzy fifteen hundred dollars."

"Fifteen hundred? Wow."

"Long story. We'll get it all back." He fumbled through his notes. "Here's Izzy's bank account."

Clair looked at the little slip of paper. "What's the money for? He didn't rub somebody out for you, did he?"

"You have to stop reading those cheap detective novels, Clair." Scott called Hope. "Hope! Put the address amount in Fellows's new account."

He read Hope the number as Clair put away her novel. "They usually require real, actual money. You know that, don't you?"

"We're following the money. Long story. I have to call Nick." Scott called.

"Another long story," she said.

Nick was delighted to have the number. "That's just outstanding, Scott. I'll start the necessary paperwork to freeze his assets."

"How long will that take, Nick?"

"Maybe a day or two. Why?"

"Well . . . it's probably better for both of us if you don't know why, Nick. Anyway, a day or two should be enough time."

"Ahh, jeez." Nick felt his stomach drop. "Don't break any laws," he said, hung up, and chewed a handful of Tums.

Jim was standing in the door again. "That was Scott Moss, Nick?"

"He just gave us a tip on Jason Fellows."

"It sounded like he broke the law to do it?"

"We don't know that, Jim. Besides, you just heard me tell him not to." Nick slowly rubbed his forehead. "And now I know why Somersby was always so irritated with him."

"Anything I can do?" Jim asked.

"Yeah, there is." Nick handed Jim the account number on the way out the door. "You can get started on freezing this account. It belongs to that Jason Fellows."

~~~~~~~~~~

Jason checked his new account, blinked, and threw his new computer across the room. Hope had managed to deposit an amount the same as his old house number. "Son of a bitch!" he screamed. The computer hit a padded chair and bounced onto the floor. He picked it up and was both relieved and angry that it still worked. He stared at the screen and slowly started rocking. "You're going to die tonight, you miserable son of a bitch." Jason took a breath, grabbed his pistol, and left his hotel room.

~~~~~~~~~~

Scott called Julia from his office. "Hey, Jules. I may have to work late tonight. How about meeting me at SushiMas for an early dinner?"

She checked her watch. "I could eat. When?"

"See you there in half an hour." Scott hung up and called Nick. "Hey, Nick, I just rattled Jason's cage a little bit. I don't know where he is, but if he looks at his numbered account it's a good guess he's going to see a new amount and overreact."

Nick held his head for a full minute before he spoke. "Please don't tell me you stole money from him, Scott. You're breaking so many laws I won't be able to keep you out of prison."

"No, no, no. I'm putting money in. That's not against the law, is it?"

"What! What the hell are you doing that for?"

"We're putting in amounts that he'll recognize. We just put his old house number in. That way he'll know we're on to him. Is there any way you can watch what he does, electronically?"

"We? Who's *we*?"

"I mean I—just me. You and me are the we." Scott cringed at his slip-up. "And it's whom."

"Yeah, right. We can't see what he's doing or where he is by his account, Scott, just how much goes in or comes out. I'm trying to freeze his actions by freezing his account and you're making a stupid deposit! Poor people are much easier to catch than rich ones." Nick sighed in frustration. "What the hell are you trying to do? Make him richer than he already is?"

"I'm trying to rattle him, Nick. Rattled people make mistakes. And we're—I mean, I'm—using the money he left here in his old accounts. If he gets angry enough he'll screw up."

"How the hell are you getting his money?"

"Do you really want to know, Nick?"

"No." Nick rubbed his forehead. "You're right, I don't. But if he moves his account again because of you and we lose him, I'm coming after you!"

"Hey! I'm the one who gave you the number."

"And you're going to give me a heart attack next!" Nick slammed the phone down. "Dammit!"

Scott met Julia, and they had a nice dinner. Julia headed for home and Scott went back to his office.

Julia sat down at her computer when she got home, felt a chill and looked around. "Hello?" She got up and listened carefully. She looked down the hall to their bedroom as she edged her way through the living room, grabbed her purse, and slipped out the door. She immediately called Scott. "Scott, I could be imagining things but I suddenly felt very uncomfortable at home. It felt like someone was there or had been there. I can't explain it."

"Go directly to your cousin's, Jules. I'll be right there. If we've been robbed I'll call the police. Go right now, okay?"

"I'm already out," she said.

"I'm headed back. I'll be there in ten minutes."

"Then I'm going to wait for you out front."

"Just go to your cousin's!"

"No thanks."

"Dammit!" Scott hung up and raced home.

Scott pulled up out front and pulled out his roll of quarters. "Did anybody come out?"

"No. Just people we know."

"You stay here." Scott went up the steps.

195

"Yeah, right." Julia followed.

"Whatever happened to dutiful wives?" Scott asked as he got to their door.

"They disappeared in the eighteenth century."

"Well, stay outside, at least." Scott readied his quarters and stepped inside.

Julia stood in the doorway while Scott roamed their apartment. "It's okay, Jules, you can come in," he said. "But you were right."

"You felt it, too?"

"No. But I can see it." Scott pointed to his desk. "Everything's been moved around a little." He checked his computer and smiled. "He dumped all the files on himself. But I have a hard copy, and Hope still has it all, too."

"Hmmm." Julia checked her desk. "I can't tell. Everything's just as messy as it always is."

"Doesn't matter. You're spending a couple of days at your cousin's. Pack a bag."

"How the heck did he find us?" Julia packed an overnight in a hurry.

"It was easy, we're in the book." Scott took a breath. "Shit! Clair's still at the office." He called. "Clair! Get the hell out of there right now!"

"On my way." Clair tossed her detective novel and grabbed her purse. When Clair got to the elevators she asked, "What am I running from?"

Julia held the door. "Let's go!"

Scott ran out of their apartment, still on the line with Clair. "Maybe nothing. But maybe Jason Fellows." He raced to his Mustang. Julia ran for her Buick.

"The creep who drowned his wife?"

"Very likely. Are you safe?"

"On the elevator, going to the first floor."

"Stay on the line until you get outside." He roared off, smoking the tires.

Julia headed for her cousin Barry's.

"Okay, I'm in the lobby, headed outside." As Clair exited the building she saw people in the coffee shop on the corner. "I'll be in the coffee shop on our corner. There's a whole bunch of people in there."

"Good. I'll be there in fifteen minutes."

"Take your time. I'm going to have pie."

"Pie?"

"It calms me down." Clair hung up.

"Best secretary—ever." Scott called Nick as he neared his office. "Hey, Nick, I think Jason Fellows took the bait. I think I pissed him off enough, that he's coming after me."

"You piss everybody off, Scott. Most of the time you don't even have to try." Nick grabbed his jacket and strapped on his weapon. "Where the hell are you?"

"I'm in my car and I'm almost to my office. I'll meet you there—step on it."

"Don't go in. Wait for me."

"I'll leave the door open. Just in case he shows up before you do." Scott closed his phone.

"Dammit!" Nick started running for his car. "If he would just do what I asked—one time!"

Jason Fellows had been sitting in his rented car, across the street, getting up the courage to kill

Scott. He had watched Clair come out and go into the coffee shop. Fifteen minutes later he watched Scott skid up and run inside. He sat for another five minutes. "Okay, you miserable prick this is it." He started to get out of his car when Nick raced up, pulled his weapon, and ran inside. "Shit!" he screamed. He watched Clair leave the coffee shop and follow Nick inside. "You sons 'a bitches," he growled, and drove off.

Nick slowly pushed Scott's unlocked door open, with the barrel of his weapon. "Scott?"

Scott was sitting at his desk behind the screen that hid him from the door. "Nick?"

Scott raised his weapon as Nick peeked around the screen, pointing his weapon. They were barrel to barrel. "Hey, Nick," Scott said softly. "Nice of you to drop by."

"Hey, Scott. I was in the neighborhood, thought I'd stop in and say hello." Nick holstered his gun. "I take it he hasn't shown up yet."

Scott set his gun on the desk. "Not yet. I can't say for sure he's coming here. But he was at our apartment, so it's a good bet."

"Well, I'm not waiting for him in your stinky darkroom closet. I'll wait down the hall. Just around the corner, at the end."

Clair cleared her throat. Both Nick and Scott grabbed their weapons and spun around. "Bang bang, you're both dead," she said dryly. She was standing next to the screen. "The killer's not gonna knock, you know."

"Don't do that!" Nick gulped.

"Good God. You scared the crap out of me," Scott said, shaking his head. "You could have been shot, Clair—by both of us."

"I have it on good authority the secretary never gets shot," she said.

Nick looked at Scott.

"She reads cheap detective novels," Scott said.

"Ten bucks isn't cheap," she retorted.

"You can't be here," Nick said.

"Why not? Won't it look suspicious if someone isn't at the front desk?"

"Clair's got a point," Scott said and looked at Nick. "Things should look normal, right?"

"No," Nick answered. "Things can go back to normal tomorrow or the next day. If Jason Fellows is anywhere near here, Clair can't be. He's a stone cold killer. We just got word that the body of a Mr. McDonnell washed up on a beach near Seattle."

"The chief steward. He's thorough." Scott said.

"Fine, I'll go home," Clair said. "But I still get paid for the day, right, Scott?"

"Yes, Clair, full pay. Go home," Scott sighed. "And it's a good guess the fake wife is dead, too."

"She'll turn up," Nick said with certainty.

Nick would be right—in a couple of years.

Scott and Nick waited until an hour past sunset before they called it a night. "I'm sorry, Nick. Maybe it was just Jules's and my own imagination getting away from us."

"Maybe I should assign some protection for you and Julia for a little while."

199

"No. Jules went to stay with her cousin, and I'm fine. But thanks anyway."

~~~~~~~~~~

Jason sat in the hotel bar, quietly fuming. Four martinis later everything in his life was a blur.

The waiter approached and startled him. "Sir?"

"Shit! What?" Jason stared, wide-eyed.

"Do you need a cab, sir? We're closing," the waiter said. "Or do you have a room here?"

"Hell, yeah, I've got a room. Do you?"

"No, sir. Do you want the tab on your room?"

"No." He paid his bill with cash and staggered up to his room. He woke up in the morning with an enormous pounding headache. "Ahhh! Jesus! Damn you, Moss, you miserable piece of crap!"

~~~~~~~~~~

Scott woke up in the morning, alone. He took the gun from under his pillow and looked at Jules's empty side of the bed. "Damn you, Fellows, you rotten bastard." He put his gun in the soap dish and took a shower.

Julia came down to breakfast in her cousin's house. "Hey, Amy. Thanks for putting me up."

"Hey, Jules. Barry's already gone to work. How about some coffee?"

"Yes, please. But let me buy you breakfast. It's the least I can do."

"Okay. Do you like huevos rancheros? There's a nice Mexican restaurant nearby—Garcia's."

Julia hesitated. "Do they have anything with fewer calories? I'm trying to keep my figure."

"Barry always gets scrambled eggs with green chile and cheese over. That's pretty light and really good. But you look great."

"It's a constant battle, Amy. Can I get it without the cheese?"

"Sure, but it won't be as good. Get dressed, skinny. I'll drive."

Scott left for work early to be sure to get there before Clair. He had his gun lying on the desk when she came in.

"Don't shoot, it's me," she said dryly. She could see his weapon through the hinge fold in the screen.

The morning came and went without incident. Scott decided to take a case involving infidelity. He hated them the most, but they paid the most. He offered to buy lunch, but Clair brought a sandwich.

"Don't open this, Clair. I'll be back in a bit." He closed the door and locked it.

Fellows watched Scott lock Clair in and leave.

Scott made the drive to SushiMas, his favorite sushi restaurant. "Hey, Mas," he said as he entered. "Two California rolls, please."

"How lookie man like married life?" Mas asked.

"Difficult to say. Our honeymoon was cut short by a murder.

"So, same, same."

"And the killer may be trying to kill Jules and me. We haven't been together much."

"Still, same, same." Mas hid a hint of a smile.

"Thanks, Mas," Scott replied, smiling himself. "I needed a good laugh about now. Did you know that the detective business really stinks?"

"You think stinks—you smell my dumpster." Mas winked. He set a square plate in front of Scott. It wasn't California roll—it never was when Scott ordered it—it was an explosion of odd pieces of raw fish, arranged in an artful pattern, green stuff and rice. It was their little game. "Enjoy," he said.

"Perfect, another mystery." Scott dug in.

~~~~~~~~~~

Fellows stood at the end of the hall, waiting for Scott to return. He would wait for the elevator doors to open, duck back around the corner, and then peek out to see if it was Scott. Four peeks and Scott finally stepped off the lift. As Scott started to unlock his office door, Fellows quickly marched up. Scott heard and sensed him more than he actually saw him. He put his hand in his pocket and gripped his roll of quarters, but Fellows stopped a good four feet short of him. He had his hand in his jacket, pointing an obvious weapon at Scott. "Stairs," was all he said.

"Door," was Scott's answer. Then Scott pointed to the ceiling. "Light," he said.

"I'll shoot you right here if I have to, you son of a bitch. Stairs!" he commanded and stabbed the gun inside his jacket, pointing to the end of the hall.

"Fine. Stairs." Scott headed for the stairs. He opened the door—labeled "Open to Street Only—" released his quarters, and got ready. As Fellows followed him through, Scott grabbed the hand inside Fellows's jacket and yanked him through, flinging him toward the flight of stairs.

The gun went off, "BLAM!" blowing a hole in his pocket. The bullet punched a hole in the center of the *O* in the *FOUR* painted on the stairwell wall, and Fellows tumbled down the stairs head-first.

"Bulls-eye'" Scott said, and started after him. He took two steps down, but Fellows had managed to wrestle his hand out of his jacket. "Uh-oh." Scott ran back up the two stairs and tried the door. It had closed and locked. He ran up for the fifth floor as Fellows fired again, "BLAM!" and missed.

The shot and echo in the stairwell was so huge that Scott covered his ears. "Damn that's loud." He pulled out his phone as he raced to the sixth floor. "Clair, take the elevator up to the twelfth floor and open the stairwell door!"

"Why? And what was that huge bang?"

"Because I don't want to have to run up twenty-four flights. The bang was a gun going off. Fellows has me trapped in the stairwell and he's shooting at me with his damn gun."

Clair was quickly in the hall, and punching the elevator button. "I think I can hear the elevator coming, hang on." She yelled.

"BLAM, BLAM!" The noise was deafening.

Clair jumped and cried, "Scott!" as the elevator doors opened.

"Better make it thirteen," Scott said, puffing. "I'm already at eight."

"There is no thirteen! And I already pushed twelve!" she cried.

"It'll have to do. Thanks, kiddo." Scott kept running. "It's gonna be tight."

Fellows was puffing up the stairs, bleeding from his nose and from a cut over his eye. "BLAM!" He fired at Scott's disappearing figure.

Clair pounded the wall. "Don't stop, don't stop, please don't stop."

Scott covered his ears. "It'll be close—open twelve. I'll try to slow him down." Scott stepped back into the line of fire and fired his roll of quarters at Fellows. Fellows ducked and fell as he fired again. "BLAM!" The quarters hit him square on top of his head and exploded—quarters flew everywhere. "Arrrrgh! Dammit!"

"Another bulls-eye." Scott pointed at Fellows.

"You bastard!" Fellows struggled to get up, stepped on the loose coins, slipped and smacked his knee on the edge of a step. "Aaggh!"

Scott quickly raced two flights ahead. Fellows recovered and stormed up the stairs, growling.

Scott slowed down at eleven to give Fellows another shot.

Fellows took the bait. "BLAM!"

Scott ducked away, and was quickly up the last flight to twelve. He wiggled the door handle. "Come on, come on, Clair. Open up."

Clair finally got to the twelfth floor and opened the stairwell. As she opened it, Scott zipped out just as Fellows rounded the stairs beneath him. Scott shoved Clair out of harm's way, left the door ajar, and got ready.

Clair slid across the floor on her bottom. "Ow! That hurt, buster."

Fellows started to open the door, slowly.

Scott waited until it started to swing open. Then he threw his full body weight into it as hard as he could. "BLAM!" Fellows's gun went off for the eighth time and he went backward again, tumbling down the stairs.

Scott carefully opened the door and peeked in. Fellows was lying, crumpled and bleeding, on the landing below. He raised his weapon. "Click"

"I was pretty sure that was eight." Scott smiled. "I'll bet that hurt just as much as the first flight you went down, didn't it?" He slowly and deliberately started walking down the stairs toward him.

Clair peeked in through the door, rubbing her bottom. "Be careful, Scott."

"He's out. No worries."

Fellows stumbled up, screamed, "You son of a bitch!" and struggled back down the stairs on his banged up knee.

Scott waved to Clair, "Go! Call the police. He's headed back down to the street. It's the only open exit. I'll follow him to make sure he doesn't double back." He kicked at his quarters on the way down the stairs. "There's ten bucks I'll never get back. Hurry up, Clair. And call the police!"

"I'm sure somebody's already called them. You could hear those shots all over the building," she hollered, and headed for the elevator.

Fellows stumbled down the stairs, trying each door as he passed. Scott followed, deliberately not catching up. People were out in the hallways, wondering what was happening. Fellows tried the fifth floor door and continued on. A man opened the fifth floor door to see who wiggled it. Fellows ran back, shoved the man out of the way, and punched the elevator button. He was a scary sight, blood all over his face. Fellows turned and pointed his empty weapon at the startled man.

"Don't shoot! I've got three kids." The man held his hands out and backed down the hall and into his office.

The elevator door opened, and Fellows stepped in. Clair was standing inside. She rolled her eyes and groaned, "Ahh, crap."

The doors closed and opened again on four. "This is where I get off," she said, drolly, and tried to get around him.

He grabbed her, punched lobby, and said, "No! You're coming with me."

"Hey! Don't get any of that blood on my blouse. I just had it cleaned," she warned.

Sirens could be heard as Jason forced Clair out of the elevator on the first floor. The police were at the front door by the time Fellows had Clair halfway down the hall. He put the empty gun to her head. "I'll kill her!" he screamed. "I mean it! I'll blow her brains out!"

The police drew their weapons, took defensive positions, and stopped. "Drop the weapon!"

"He's out!" Clair yelled. "Come on, get him!"

"Release the woman!" the sergeant demanded.

As Fellows backed down the hall, Scott opened the stairway door. He stepped out between the police and Fellows.

Fellows had put his arm around Clair's neck. "Stay away or I'll kill her! I'll kill her!"

The sergeant frantically screamed, "Hey you, move! Get down! Get out of the line of fire!"

Scott looked back and forth.

"He's out!" Clair yelled. "He's out!"

"Get out of the way!" the sergeant hollered.

Scott patted the air. "It's okay. I got this."

Wild-eyed, Fellows backed up to the corner, against the wall. "I'll kill her!" he screamed. "I'm not kidding! I'll kill her!"

"Get down!" Sarge yelled, as desperate and wild-eyed as Fellows. "Get out of the way!"

"I'll kill her!" Fellows repeated.

"Get down dammit!" the sergeant screamed.

Scott walked up to Jason, smiling. "You heard Clair. You're out." He punched Jason Fellows in his already broken nose with his fist.

Fellows' head bounced off the back wall, and he slid, straight down, unconscious. The cops flew in and kicked his gun away.

"Thanks a lot," Clair said dryly.

Scott gently said, "You're okay, you're okay." And gave her a hug.

She let him hug her. "I'm fine, Scott. I knew his gun was empty." Her hands were at her sides and she patiently stared at the ceiling.

He kept holding her. "It's okay, it's okay."

Clair indifferently endured his hug for as long as she could. Finally she said, "I'm not going to have to file sexual harassment charges against you, am I?" in the driest of voices.

Scott let go and led her away from the action. "You're something else."

The cops were all over Jason Fellows. "What went on here?" the sergeant asked.

"He's wanted for murder," Scott said.

"What happened to his face? Why did you beat him up?" the cop asked.

"He's wanted by the FBI. He committed a crime up in Alaska."

"So you beat the hell out of him?"

"No. He tried to shoot me, and I had to throw him down the stairs," Scott said, and pointed to the hole in Jason's jacket.

"Ohh." The sergeant nodded. "And?"

"He killed his wife and dumped her in the river. The FBI's been looking for him for over a month."

"The LA River?" The sergeant looked confused.

"A river up in Alaska."

"Not here?"

"No."

"Okay. Good to know," the cop said.

"The funny thing is, he actually got away with it. We couldn't find him anywhere, but he came back to kill me. If he'd just stayed where he was he'd probably be free forever."

"Why'd he want to kill you?" the cop asked.

"Doesn't everybody?" Clair muttered.

The cop frowned. "What?"

"Long story." Scott shrugged. "I purposely got under his skin to smoke him out."

"Ahhh! Look at that." Clair pulled out her collar to see. It had Jason's blood all over it. She glared at Scott. "You owe me a new blouse," she said, and marched to the elevator.

"That your mother?" the cop asked.

Clair stood, rubbing her collar and fussing.

Scott grinned as he answered, "Almost. She's my secretary."

"We'll need her statement," the sergeant said.

Scott handed him his business card. "We're on the fourth floor. Give her a minute to calm down."

"Hey, I know you," one of the cops said. "You got Bendouski. Right?"

"I helped." Scott got on his phone. "Hey, Nick. Fellows came back today—to kill me."

Nick sat bolt upright. "Where is he now?"

"The LAPD has him. We're at my office."

"Is everybody okay?" he asked.

"Yeah. But Clair's got Jason's blood all over her blouse. She's really mad at me."

"Blood? On Clair? Is she okay? Was he shot? No, you don't have to tell me." Nick shook his head. "You gotta stop punching people, Scott."

"Hey! Why do you . . ."

"Never mind. Just let me talk to the officer in charge, okay?"

Scott handed the sergeant his phone. "This is Special Agent Nick Scraper, of the FBI. He asked to speak to you."

While the sergeant and Nick talked, Scott went up and apologized to Clair.

Nick and Jim eventually showed up and took charge of Jason Fellows.

Scott called Julia when the commotion died down. "Hey, Jules, we were right. Fellows *was* in town. Nick has him in custody."

Julia was silent for a full minute.

"Jules?"

"So where are we going on our honeymoon, Scott?" Julia asked. "And not Mexico."

Novels by Ross Van Dusen

Heavenly Hash. Doug Ribbons runs a candy factory. He has to find a way to keep 100 pounds of Marijuana-laced chocolate out of circulation.

Burgle Back. Brad Portman has a neighbor's stolen merchandise in his garage. He tries to burgle it back before he's implicated in his neighbor's crimes.

Area 102. Four scientists get an assignment that lets them know their Army careers are over. With no résumé possible because of the secrecy of their work, they decide to get even.

R&R. Three Germans stuck inside their broken tank—in an Italian village. Four GI's surround the tank. Two prostitutes come and go, at will.

Where's Mrs. Bendouski? *#1 The Scott Moss detective series.* Scott Moss is sure mob boss Tony Bendouski killed Mrs. Bendouski, but has no proof.

Who's the Dead Guy? *#2 The Scott Moss detective series.* Scott Moss takes a fuzzy photo of a man being thrown off a roof. The body disappears, and no one believes there really was a crime.

What About Zerovsky's Brother? *#3 The Scott Moss detective series.* Scott Moss finds a dead man in the theatre—Zerovsky. Who killed him? And what does his twin brother have to do with it?

Who Killed Scooter Diamond? *#4 The Scott Moss detective series.* It looked like an accident, but Scott Moss has promised to help the jockey's wife, Hope, prove Scooter Diamond was murdered.

Where Did Everybody Go? *#5 The Scott Moss detective series.* Scott Moss and his fiancée Julia Weston go to SushiMas to plan their wedding. The trip ends in a hail of bullets.

Who Stabbed Reverend Wicker? *#6 The Scott Moss detective series.* Scott and Julia plan to get married in her church. But her minister is stabbed before they can set the date.

Who's At The Bottom Of The River? *#7 The Scott Moss detective series.* Scott takes his bride, Julia, on a honeymoon cruise in Alaska. A murder on board the boat turns the trip into an international manhunt.

Ross Van Dusen writes fast-paced action comedy novels perfect for the beach, airplane, bed, or anywhere you need a laugh.

www.rossvandusen.com
www.rossvandusenblog.blogspot.com

Made in the USA
Columbia, SC
17 September 2024

41992091R00124